More praise for JUNIOR RAY

"Mississippi tourist officials won't be handing this book out anytime soon, though they might be surprised by its effectiveness if they did . . . Not for the squeamish, but its irreverent humor will win over most." — *Publishers Weekly*

"For all Junior Ray's ugly talk, the writing here is beautifully crafted. Providing counterpoint to Junior Ray's perfectly calibrated invective, Pritchard sprinkles the narrative with Leland Shaw's heartbreaking journal entries about being hunted by Nazis . . . while not for the squeamish, [Junior Ray] deserves shelf space beside the best southern literature—even if it makes its neighbors blush." — BARNES & NOBLE

"Junior Ray is an unforgettable narrator: hilarious, rowdy, and stubbornly his own. In life you'd cross the street to avoid him; in Pritchard's delightful fictional debut, you'll turn the pages to see what that rascal does next." — LOUISE REDD, *Hangover Soup*

"Junior Ray Loveblood has taken profanity and made a new language of it, which he uses to tell the often hilarious, often scary, story of life as a poor white in the Mississippi Delta, down its lonely roads and through its dark forests. Not for the squeamish or pure at heart." — JOHN FERGUS RYAN, *White River Kid*

"A whizbang of a book—funny, eccentric in that great Southern tradition, pitch-perfect, and beautifully paced. Junior Ray's voice, while repugnant, is also beguiling, sorrowful—though he doesn't know it—and rich in cracker surrealism. The book drips with Delta air and brings alive its peculiar, specific population." — BURKE'S BOOKSTORE

"Mark Twain meets the Coen Brothers in this foul-mouthed farce. This short burst of a novel reads like a delicious white trash tirade, bound to offend but a whole lot of demented fun." — SQUARE BOOKS

ALSO BY JOHN PRITCHARD
The Yazoo Blues

JUNIOR RAY

JOHN PRITCHARD

NEWSOUTH BOOKS
Montgomery | Louisville

NewSouth Books
P.O. Box 1588
Montgomery, AL 36102

Library of Congress Cataloging-in-Publication Data

Pritchard, John, 1938-
Junior Ray / John Pritchard.
p. cm.
ISBN-13: 978-1-58838-232-0 (pbk.)
ISBN-10: 1-58838-232-X (pbk.)
1. Rednecks--Fiction. 2. Rednecks--Attitudes--Fiction. 3. Delta (Miss. : Region)--
Fiction. 4. Mississippi--Fiction. 5. Satire. I. Title.
PS3616.R5725J86 2008
813'.6--dc22

2008040562

Design by Randall Williams
Printed in the United States of America

To Cele

CONTENTS

INTERVIEWER'S COMMENT

THIS BOOK IS NOT FOR THE SQUEAMISH, YET IT IS ESSENTIAL reading for those who wish to understand the Mississippi Delta, its conflicts of class and race, its angels and, most certainly, its demons.

It was in my investigation of this peculiar region that I made two significant discoveries: (1) that the *Notebooks of Leland Shaw* did exist and (2) that they were in the possession of a Mr. Junior Ray Loveblood, of whom my mother had heard much from my uncle, the late Owen Glyndwyr Brainsong, formerly the Superintendant of Education for Mhoon County.

I was informed by the grandson of a Mr. Mudd that Mr. Loveblood had Shaw's diaries—works of supposed literary merit, which, frankly, I had consigned to the closet of local mythology, or at least to the same category as that of the "works" of Professor Floodwater Scott whose famous footlockers everyone believed to be filled with his detailed record of the Southern oral tradition . . . turned out to be totally oral.

The thing is, I understood instantly the magnitude of the journals I discovered to be, in fact, in Mr. Loveblood's possession—and I think Uncle Owen would have agreed. Namely, that just as Walter Anderson was the great Artist of the Mississippi Coast, so Leland Shaw might well be—or have been—the *other* great Poet of the Mississippi Delta. I hasten to assure the reader that I do not for a single moment mean to diminish the literary contribution and stature of William Alexander Percy. Indeed, though both Percy and Shaw were regional and cultural countrymen, neighbors, in fact, I can see nowhere that their work conflicts even in the slightest.

"Good God!" I had said to myself. "I must obtain those Notebooks!" Thus, I went to see Mr. Loveblood—or Junior Ray, as I came to know him.

He was not hard to find, and it turned out that what I had been told was true. I have now seen, first hand, *The Notebooks of Leland Shaw*, and, throughout the text of the interview, samples are provided for the reader. The mystery is why Junior Ray kept them all these years, when, after knowing anything at all about Junior Ray, one might easily have assumed he would have used them for kindling.

I know now that to have thought so would be to misapprehend the make-up of and to grossly underestimate possibly one of the most complex and perhaps genuinely archetypal characters ever to have lived in that most distinctive part of the deep American South. Yet, even in Junior Ray's loud insistence, in reference to Shaw's *Notebooks*, that "They ain't nothin but a pile of crap," he makes it quite clear he has no intention of giving up his ownership of Shaw's work. And so I became acquainted with a genuine enigma, Junior Ray Loveblood, and it was from him, finally, that I decided to learn as much as I could, from his rather unrestrained perspective, about the Delta.

On the face of it, choosing Junior Ray as an informant might have seemed an odd option for a serious scholar, such as I, in the field of Anthropological Philology; yet, I have observed that among all the rigorous disciplines, flexibility is a virtue, and, most assuredly, opportunity is its reward. As I saw it, I stood to benefit doubly by having access to Shaw's "Notes" as well as— how shall I put it . . . also to Shaw's antithesis, Junior Ray Loveblood. In that way, I believed I might obtain a most unusual three-dimensional grasp of the region.

It is of the utmost importance that I communicate to you, the reader, that my interest in Shaw's "Notes," both as literature and as record, was actually secondary to my curiosity about the place; for it was the place, I felt, that had made Shaw, and from that point of view, it seemed to follow that it was in fact the place that had really produced the "Notes." Suddenly I understood. In the single powerful and didactic moment of an instinctual epiphany, I saw that the place had two voices. One was that of Shaw. The other was Junior Ray's. The situation was unique, and I embraced it.

Junior Ray was not easy to interview. At first he didn't want to do it, but after we began, as time went on, he seemed to enjoy the attention, so I did not rein him in, as one or two others suggested I should do for sake of propriety.

Instead I sat quietly and took down all he had to tell me about Leland Shaw and about that time and place. I recorded as accurately as I could all he said, precisely the way he said it. The text that follows consists of Junior Ray's narrative interspersed with selected excerpts from Shaw's "Notes," so that the reader can indeed hear the two voices, those of Junior Ray and Leland Shaw, as separate realities of a single illusion: that mythical place Mississippians know as The Delta.

— OWEN G. BRAINSONG II

JUNIOR RAY

I

ME — LELAND SHAW — VOYD — TEMPTATION
JONES — SUNFLOWER'S UNDERPANTS

SOME PEOPLE MIGHT SAY THERE AIN'T MUCH TO ME, BUT that's a gotdamn lie. There's just as much to me as it is to any other sumbich I know. Yeah, maybe I wouldn't be here doing what I'm doing if I'da handled a few things different, way back yonder, but I can't change none of that now.

I guess I started head'n down the wrong road about the time that crazy-ass sumbich Leland Shaw run off from the "Rest Wing" of the county hospital and hid out in old Miss Helena Ferry's silo for about three months in the winter of nineteen fifty-nine. I wanted to kill him then, and, if he was alive today—and I guess he might be—I'd want to kill him now, and I do. Hell, being able to kill him and get away with it was the whole point of the thing. I can't explain it. It's just something about him I hate, and, quite frankly, if you want to know the truth, I really kinda enjoy the feeling, even though it didn't start out in that fashion: I didn't hate him at first. In fact, in the beginning I didn't have no feeling about him one way or the other. He was just what you might call *convenient*, a sumbich I could shoot and have it looked on as a public service. And that particular set of circumstances would have allowed me to do what I had always wanted to do, namely, shoot the shit out of somebody. But, as time went by, things changed, or at least the way I felt about him did, so that I ended up hating him and couldn't really say why. I just did, and then it seemed like I ought to have been hating his ass all along only I hadn't known to do it. Well, as I always say, live and fukkin learn.

Though, *personally*, if I couldn't no longer get a rush out of hating the memory of Leland Shaw—and one or two others connected with him—like that high-yellow bitch that come back down here from Chicago that time—I wouldn't see no sense in living.

I know you probably think I'm an asshole, and maybe I am, but I don't give a damn. I didn't then, and I don't now. And if I ever see one of them coksukkin Mohammedan muthafukkas again, or whatever they call theysefs, I'mo do him like my daddy and them done his ancestors back in Clay City, over in the hills, when I was a *little* fukka. They had a sign up across't the main street there that said, "NIGGA, DON'T LET THE SUN SET ON YOUR BLACK ASS IN CLAY CITY." By god them ol' boys meant it, and that's why Clay City is where it is today.

They all say the Delta's different, and it is, too. When I got here forty-odd years ago, the Delta wuddn nothin like where I come from. But, hell, I hear this little old Delta town right here was just as bad in some ways as Clay City, like the time back around 1910 when that northern girl's father got off the train and saw two bucks hangin' from the telegraph poles and then come to find out they was three more of 'em hangin' off that big old scalybark set'n there beside Charlie Hayes's driveway; but, of course, it wuddn nothin' there then but the tree and a little bit of woods. Later on, the story was that whoever did the hangin' was after a white fellow, too, but he got away, natcherly. And It wuddn no nightklux what done it—them planters here in the county wouldna put up with that—it was just a buncha town folks that went out and got them niggas and hanged 'em. I sure don't know what for, and they probably wuddn too sure about it neither. You know how it is when things get started. But Christ almighty, it wuddn no big thing back in them times. Hell, you're just talkin' about four or five dead niggas. 'Course, I hear some of them big planters didn't see it thataway. You can understand it when you realize how important niggas was to *them* in those days. Hell, they couldn't get along unless they had a whole house full of 'em. Then, too, them planters liked to be the ones who controlled things, and a lotta times, so I hear, they and some of the merchants in the town didn't always see eye to eye—like when the klan wanted to come in and some of the merchants wanted to let 'em. Them planters put a stop to that real quick. Well, I mean, they owned the land and near 'bout everybody on it, so why shouldn't they be the ones to run the show? And it wuddn all bad neither. But that was a another time, and just like anything else, it had its pluses and minuses.

Anyhow, I am no worse than most and not as bad as some, though, Lord knows, I've tried. I ain't afraid to say what I think, and if some bigshot sumbich don't like it, fukkim.

I said a minute ago "if Leland Shaw was alive." The fact is, he might be. We never caught him, but I did see him, and the last time—or so I will always believe—was in the car with them Mohammedans later that day when the whole thing suddenly come to an end over at Miss Helena Ferry's house. I'll have to get into that directly and, also, that business about the submarine and us meetin' up with them Boy Sprouts out behind the levee. There was a-lots of things I didn't understand and, even now, can't make much sense out of. But it was a wild time, I'll say that. And me and my old buddy Voyd loved almost every minute of it.

NOW, LET ME JUST SAY one thing—maybe two—right here. First, I don't mind being interviewed and talking about what happened, but I want to get something straight on the front end: All this has got to be wrote the way I tell it.

And second, the other thing you wanted to know about was them "Notebooks." I'll get to them in a minute—

I DON'T SEE MUCH of Voyd no more, not since he had his bypass. And then, too, he got married—married Sunflower LeFlore and farmed for a number of years on her daddy's place. I remember when I let him borrow my patrol car—I was a deputy sheriff at the time—so he and Sunflower could go out on a turnrow somewhere. She got drunk and pissed all over the front seat of the official vehicle and then passed out.

I could've gotten in trouble for that. But Sheriff Holston never did find out—or if he did, he never let on—and everything worked out okay. If anything had been said about it, I was just going to claim I forgot to put the window up and a cat got in the car. It really didn't smell much like cat piss, but I figured it was close enough to satisfy the average person.

I was real young and didn't think out what I was doing before I did it. And I was a lot carefuler after that, because I realized how much my job meant to me, and I didn't want to lose it. Seemed like I was meant to be a deputy and I had found my place in the world. But, now, old Voyd and me was real close. He wuddn even a deputy, but he was with me all the time and might as well have been. He had a little refrigerator repair business, but he worked at it so seldom, I swear, I think he about forgot how to do it. Sunflower, well, she was always the kinda girl that keeps her panties in her purse. You know what I mean. Voyd, though, he was blind as a bat to all that. You know love. When it bites a sumbich he either can't or won't see shit, or worse, he sees stuff that ain't there and drives himself nuts and ever'body else around him. Anyhow, one day Voyd comes up to me and says, "Junior Ray, I got to ast you somethin." And I said, "What is it, Voyd?"

He said, "Somethin's botherin' me."

"Like what?" I said.

"Like Sunflower's underpants," he said.

"What about her underpants?" I ast him, knowing sure as shoot'n what he was gon' tell me.

"They was in her purse," he said.

Playin' dumb, I said, "Well, at least, they was in HER purse."

"What the fuk does that mean!" he hollered and then said, "Gotdammit, Junior Ray, be serious."

"All right," I said. "How come they was in her purse?"

"Well," says Voyd, "I ast her; I said, 'Sunflow'r, how come you got your underpants in your purse?' And she said, 'Well, Voyd, it *is* the middle of *summer!*' And I ast her if all ladies carried their underpants around with 'em in their purses in the middle of summer, and she said, 'How the fuk would I know! I don't go around lookin' in their purses like some people around here. That's the dumbest question I ever heard.'"

Then I asked Voyd what she finally gave him as the whole excuse, and he said, "Well, she said she did it as a way to *com*-bat the heat." According to Voyd, he looked her straight in the eye and said, "Gotdamn, Sunflow'r, how fukkin hot can it be?" Then he said she looked like she was gonna tune up and cry, and she told him she done took 'em off to be more comfortable, and then Voyd said he asked her how can them flimsy little old things be anything *but* comfortable, and she said he never did believe her and never did trust her and all that crap, and then, *Voyd,* that dumb sumbich, started feelin' sorry for her and feelin' even worse that he had brought it up in the first place, and so, finally, there that coksukka is, and he's askin' me:—"Junior Ray, you think I ought to be worried?"

"'Bout what?" I said, like I didn't know what he meant.

"'Bout Sunflow'r, you know . . ."

And I told him; I said, "Voyd, put it this way, I don't think the weather is your main concern."

"What the fuk, does that mean!" he asked me, and I said, "Voyd, if Sunflower is so hot she has to carry her panties around in her purse, then I'd say she's takin' her termperature with somebody else's thermometer."

Man, he had a fit about that, but he got over it, and I didn't say no more about it. People do what they're going to do, and that's it. I got a philosophy: things work out, or they don't.

BUT IT'S FUNNY how things change. I never did get married. Me and my old girlfriend, Des—that's short for *Desira*, who was a girl back yonder in a Flash Gordon funny book—just more or less stopped seeing one another, and then there never was nobody else special, and, I don't know, one day it just seemed like time had passed, and I hadn't paid it no 'tention. *Time*, I mean.

Now Des, she married Garvin what's-his-name from down around Dundee—last time I saw him he was cryin' and eat'n a beer bottle inside the Ole Miss Drive-Inn, a cafe which used to sit up there on the side of the road on the way to Meffis. Nothin' but an empty building there now. And it ain't got no roof.

Anyway, Garvin was upset because his first wife had run off with a flim-flam man I call "Temptation Jones." He was a fellow who come to town one day and, in the course of about a week, got all the merchants to participate in a contest and to put up merchandise as prizes, along with a good bit of cash—one hunnerd and ten dollars to be exact—which he, the flim-flam man, collected and held on to. And it was all to go to whoever could guess the identity of "Temptation Jones." Theoretically "Temptation Jones" was supposed to turn out to be one of the men downtown, but none of it was ever very clear—except the fact that, on the morning they were supposed to award the prizes to whoever had wrote down the true identity of "Temptation Jones" and was the winner of the contest, everybody waited and waited for the stranger to appear and say who won, but he never showed up, 'cause that sumbich had run off with every bit of the merchandise, all the cash, and, as it turned out, with Garvin–what's–his–name's first wife. And that was possibly the strangest thing of all. Shoot, anybody could see why the feller would want the prizes and the money, but nobody could figure out why he'd want to include Garvin's wife, because it wuddn no government secret that she was ugly enough to make a freight train take a *turnrow*. Well, hell, Garvin weren't no movie star hissef. However, he looks a lot better now that Des has took a hand to him and made him dress nice and use hair spray.

But, the truth is, a lot more was disappearing at that time than just those things. And had it not been for what's just happened around here recently, the whole gotdamn town was on its way to disappearing. It just goes to show, you can't always tell the difference between when something's ending and when it's beginning. A lot of times it looks the same.

Back to Garvin: one morning, before he got straightened out, I remember somebody cut him up real good in a fight, and he was walking right down main street in St. Leo with his arms folded in front of him holding his intestines to keep 'em from falling out on the sidewalk. And it was a good thing they didn't, too, because them was still the old days, and they'd a' been stepped on real quick. I was in the City Barber Shop, and I saw him. Say what you will, he mighta had a soft heart, but he was a tough muthafukka.

Anyway, Des got ahold of him and turned him into a solid citizen, made him to stop eat'n glass and become a member of the Lion's Club. And I hear he did pretty good sellin' insurance, which is what all them reformed muthafukkas seem to wind up doin'; and him and Des have a granddaughter over at Chickasaw West. That's in Coldwater. It's a college. Over in the Hills.

I'm just glad it was him and not me; that's all I got to say. I never did understand how a man could be married to just one woman all his life. The way I figure it is we—men that is—are more like the buffalo. By that I mean a man just naturally needs to roam the herd and service as many buffalettes as he can. That's just nature. And—now, I know them preachers would disagree, but that ain't nothin' new—I say it is contrary to the way things really are, as I see it, for a man to tie hisself down to one woman for his *en*tire lifetime—shoot, after a while he spends most of his waking moments trying to get away from her, and she nine times out of ten don't want to *do* it no more and just wants to "cuddle" or flat wants to be left alone. I be dammed if I'd want to live like that. Hell, I'm better off with cable than I would be with a woman who don't want nothin' to do with you but at the same time wants you to do everything in the world for her and who won't give you time of day much less a piece of pussy which you don't want from *her* in the first place. At least you can unplug the TV; and, even if it don't give you a lot, it don't ask nothin' of you, neither. So I say fuk bein' married.

Move, I got to spit.

And then when you *don't* want to mess with 'em, they get mad. Mean, too. I 'member one night back in, I reckon it was nineteen fifty-seven, Des and me was at the MoonLite Drive-In movie the-ater, north of Clarksdale at Lyon, and the mosquitos was chewin' us up something awful; plus it was hotter'n a bitch in heat, and I was sweat'n like a nigga on election day. Well, we'd been rolling around in the back seat the whole time, and I was get'n somewhat wore out—I mean, let's face it, you can just laugh so much. And here's what I'm talking about when I say a woman can have a mean mouth: I says to her, "You want some more milkduds?" And she says, "Damn you, Junior Ray; food's all you ever think about"—bear in mind we'd been wallowin' all over my fifty-four Chevy for a good hour and fifteen minutes; didn't neither one of us know what the movie was about, and don't to this day—and then she says, "I guess you just druther fart than fuk." Now, I'mo tell you, don't many things get away with me; but, man, that hurt.

It was awful insensitive of her if you ask me—but I suppose I can understand it to some degree, because, you see, women don't fart. Well, they do when they get to be on up in years, but, now, think about it; when's the last time you seen a young, pretty thing rip off a great big ol' crowd-dispersing poot? You never will, neither, 'cause they simply *do not fart*.

Anyhow, it was that time at the MoonLite Drive-In when I could see what it would be like if Des and me was married, and I knew then it wuddn for me. Shoot, I was fairly young then, and I intended to have me a good time without put'n up with that kind of unpleasantness. I mean, screw Clarksdale. Hell, I rather go to Meffis anyhow. And, back then you could still go to the King Cotton or any number of them other hotels and order up whatever you wanted from the bellhop and then be free to do as you please the rest of the time. Plus, you didn't have to put up with all them mosquitos.

Well, that was over forty years ago. I've calmed down a good bit since then. For some time now I been going over to Sledge to see this woman. Her husband died and left her a house, a nineteen eighty-six Coupe de Ville, one nem big-screen TVs, and six hundred acres of rice which she rents out for about sixty-five dollars an acre. With all that and social security, she lives pretty good. Hell, she ought to. She worked twenty years at the mattress factory the other side of Lambert. Anyway, her and me gets together about twice't a week, and mostly we cook out on the grill and watch *Matlock*. Once in a while, however, usually after the first frost, she fixes chittlins, and that's some good eat'n—slung or unslung, it don't matter to me, fried or boiled. When it's chittlin cookin time in Quitman County, son, I'll be there.

But, you know, as much as I love them things, I do think it is strange that so much fuss is made over a pot full of hog guts. Yet, they's just something about 'em, and once't you get hooked on 'em, you can't ever turn 'em down even when you know what they are and where they been. I just try not to think about it, but it's hard not to do when you know what you're putting in your mouth. I mean it is peculiar. I know people that would shy away from a raw oyster but wouldn't think twice about bite'n into the fricaseed asshole of a five-hundred-pound pig. If you figure it out, let me know.

I've improved a whole helluva lot since I first came here. I even go to church a good bit because, whereas I used to think God had it in for me and was after my ass, I now know that God is a god of love—and, if you don't b'lieve it, he'll burn your butt in hell for e-fukin-ternity, 'cause, you see, and here's what people don't understand, He is *also* a *just* God. Somehow, all of a sudden, everything made sense. See, there's a difference in the ways of God and the ways of men. As I say, I been goin' to church pretty regular for some years now, and I know what it means to know the Lord. Let me tell you, a sumbich don't know peace until he knows Christ. The way I figure it is, if that muthafukka came down here and died for my ass, then the only way I can thank him is by doing his will, whatever the fuk that is.

I'm a lot better about all that now than I used to be. I'm not sayin' I'm deeply spiritual. Fuk no. I'm just sayin' I'm a somewhat better individual than I was when I was real young and workin' as a deputy for Sheriff Holston. Then, I wuddn nothin' but a hunnerd-dollar gun slung on a two-bit ass. Well, that's what old Sticks Ferry called me one day. I didn't appreciate it at the time, yet I guess now that I got a few years on me, I have to agree with him. But I still didn't like the sumbich—well, hell, he didn't like me.

BACK TO LELAND SHAW, it ain't no secret that I wanted to shoot the crazy muthafukka, and that's a fact. In my opinion, it woulda been a good deed. But some of them assholes didn't see it that way, and although I didn't know it then, I can see now that that episode was probably the beginning of the end of my career as a deputy.

I never woulda gotten to be sheriff. You have to be elected to do that, and, in these Delta counties, even though things was changin' and changin' fast, back then you had to be somebody that didn't *need* to be sheriff if you wanted to be sheriff—hell, we had sheriffs around here that didn't know the first thing about law enforcement; they was cotton farmers. Although I will say this, and that is, a lot of times, back then it seemed to me we had less law and a good bit more justice. But all that's gone now. Yessir, gone with the fukkin wind.

And the same thing has happened in other parts of the state and in other states, too, so I hear. I really never traveled much—only been to Jackson five times in my whole life. Didn't think much of it, to tell you the truth. Last time I was there was in 1965, and a friend of mine and I stayed in a whorehouse down near the railroad station. Place looked like something out of a Saturday western. The room had one nem wash stands with a pitcher! But the thing that I can't help remembering is that there we wuz in that Saturday–western whorehouse, and right across the street, in the King Edward Hotel, was all them legislaytchers—you know, senators and such. And I thought about that, so that, now, lookin' back on it all, it's hard for me to say which house had the most whores.

Anyhow, the Leland Shaw thing is what I want to talk about, and I keep getting off the subject.

In a way I hated him because he was not the maniac everybody had thought he was and that I, of course, had hoped he was. You see, it was my one opportunity to really do something, and that crazy sumbich fukked it up, mainly, by not turning out to be the menace to society that, for a while, everybody believed he was and probably, like me, needed him to be. You know how people are. They want life in a small town to be something more than what it actually is. But, as you you know, what they want don't ever stay wanted.

Neverthe-fukkin-less, when it all started, it was my intention to *save* people and to do something good for the county. Then, little by little, all that changed. and I had to admit I just wanted a chance to shoot somebody. There wuddn no two ways about it.

I couldn't stand the thought of being a deputy in a sleepy little old Delta town, carrying a gun all my life and never get'n to put it to the use for which it was intended. Let's face it, a thirty-eight was not designed for hunting rabbits or for shoot'n turtles offa logs. Nor was it intended for some silly-ass target practice. It was designed for one thing and one thing only, and

I was not about to carry that side arm around all my life and not at least once't shoot the shit out of somebody.

I didn't figure I was no different from them old sumbiches in the Bible. They didn't let a day go by that they didn't run out and slay or otherwise smite somebody. In fact, the biggest smiter of 'em all was old God, hissef. Now that's one advantage of going to church all the time, I learn a lot. Turns out I ain't too much different from old Jehovah, personality-wise. 'Course, I'm the first to admit there's also some major differences, too. But if you want to know about smiting, take a look at Deuteronomy and at Joshua. Those two coksukkas were experts at it.

Now, though Leland Shaw was not—as he bygod ought to have been—dangerous, he was crazy as I don't know what. I got no sympathy with a sumbich that goes crazy in the first gotdamn place. That's one thing I had against him. He goes to war and loses his mind. Shoot, I'd about lose *my* mind if I didn't. But you probably know the story—I had a bad back . . . if it hadn't have been for that, I'da been right over there in Korea shoot'n them little slant-eyed muthafukkas and pokin' their women sideways and havin' me one helluva time. And that's just what Jehovah woulda done. I forget where he says it, but he tells the chosen people to go into a place and put all the men and boys to the sword and to take the women and the animals for themselves. If I'da knowed all that, I'da been goin' to church a lot sooner. It just goes to show that the Lord does work in mysterious ways. I'm livin' proof of that.

In fact, one time a sumbich said to me that I was *absolute* proof that there wuddn no such thing as evolution. I took that as a compliment. I guess he was some kinda preacher.

Anyhow, here's what that crazy sumbich Leland Shaw done. He comes home from the war, that's Dubbya Dubbya Two, and goes to live with his mama who was getting on up in years. It turns out he has been shellshocked or something because, even though the town put on a big celebration for him and called it WELCOME HOME LELAND SHAW DAY, he didn't seem to be too sure about what was going on. And when they asked him what he was going do now that the war was over, he said, "I'm going home." They thought he meant his mama's house.

Unh–uh. Think again, muthafukka. That sumbich was talkin' about St. Leo, the actual town itself. He, it seems, did not *believe* he was home. And that is partly what led to the whole buncha stuff that followed some time later.

You know a sumbich *is* crazy if he's set'n right there in his mama's house and don't believe he's home. But, get this, as it turned out, he not only did not believe he was home, he thought he was still over in Germany. How a sumbich could hang around here and swat these crow-size mosquitos and think he was in Europe is a mystery to me. I ain't ever been to Europe, but I read about it and I seen plenty of things about it on cable, so I know that it ain't nothin' like it is here in Mhoon County, Mississippi, in the Delta.

Nevertheless, that's the way he was. And on top of it, he believed they was some German soldiers following him around and was after him. Occasionally he would have a real spell of that, and he'd go hide. After a while, we got to where we would know where to look, and we usually was able to get him to go on back to his mama's house, where he would disappear for quite some time.

But she died, and that's when things really started to go from bad to worse. For a while, he seemed to get along okay. He worked up at the lumber company and wouldn't never say nothing to nobody—he just come to work every day, did his job, and went home, back to his mama's house. Nobody never

paid him a whole lot of attention, although some people ex-
pressed concern, sayin' they didn't know how he was going to
get along in the years to come, not havin' anybody to look after
him and all. I heard about it, but I didn't give a damn what
happened to him one way or another.

Why? I'll tell you why. Here he is, a soldier home from the
war. They give him a parade, such as might be called a parade in
St. Leo, and had a buncha people make speeches—all about how
Leland Shaw was a hero and had this and that medal give to him,
and all the time that crazy sumbich is sit'n up there on the
platform not believing for one moment that he has come home
at all, and, at that point, nobody realized he was that way. Hell,
first time I laid eyes on him when he got back, I knew he was
nuts.

And what really gets away with me is that there he was, born
with a silver spoon up his ass, his great-grandfather the founder
of the town, and him, the asshole in question—the so-called
hero—growing up a little clipped-dick sissy livin' with his
mama and daddy and them crazy old aunts of his next door. And
the worst one of them was that gotdamn nigga-lovin' Miss
Helena Ferry. She was somethin' else.

How can a sumbich like that turn out to be any crazier than
he is in the first place, much less become a coksukkin overly
decorated war hero who's done got back home and don't even
know it? I mean, even though he seemed to recognize ever'thing,
he still, somehow, didn't know where the fuk he was and didn't
believe you when you'd tell him.

Anyhow, there it was, Leland Shaw livin' what appeared to
be an all-right life day to day, yet, unbeknownst to the town, at
this point anyway, thinkin' German soldiers was following him
around trying to get him, and thinking, too, that he was still
somewhere in Europe. "Silesia" he called it. Maybe that explains

why he picked a gotdamn silo to hide out in when he run off. But there ain't no explainin' what a crazy person thinks. All I know is that sumbich ruined my life.

Well, maybe he didn't do it directly, but I'm where I am today because of him. And I don't know where, or even *if*, he is.

2

Shaw's Notebooks — Bone Face —
Shaw Runs Off — Sheep

NOW I'LL SAY SOMETHING ABOUT THEM "NOTE BOOKS" WE
found in Shaw's hidy-hole he had up there under the roof of
Miss Helena's silo. I'll show you a little bit of what that crazy-ass
muthafukka put in 'em, and I'll show you some more as we go
along. This'll give you a better understanding of what I was up
against*:

> Call it day; it is the blinding and the time when one cannot
> navigate the farther [sic] of waters; it is the time when time as
> binder and as image cannot be seen shining in the night, for, as
> I recall, time is in the light, and I am called to find the point in

---

*[Interviewer's Note to the Reader: Here Junior Ray rose from his chair and
walked into the hallway where he went to a door behind and beneath the
staircase, the usual location of the steps leading to a basement, but there are
almost no basements in Delta dwellings, for, indeed, they are already in one. He
opened the door to a deep if not large closet; then, standing on the threshold, he bent
over, rummaged about briefly but noisily and hauled forth an enormous light-
tan canvas hunting coat, of which not only the game pockets but the coat itself—
buttoned up and bound into a bundle with lengths of cotton rope—bulged and
strained at every stitch and seam with the weight of what appeared to be angular
objects. He lifted the grotesque and bloated garment from the floor of the
closet with both hands and carried it with him back to his chair in the living room

all the scattered starburst where home is racing out of reach,
where light cannot be caught except by theory and with
sighs, to be held only and forever in the arms of infinite longing, which is where I, the lone and infinite longer, may have
found my place.

About the myth, however, or the lack it,
it was in the flight and in the call of birds.
It lay in the shadows of the high grass,
and it thrummed at night
when the windows of the car were down.
It was in the silence of summer afternoons
and in the hands of Negroes who moved
like solitary dreams
above the rising heat.

------

where he dropped the swollen coat upon the floor between our two chairs. This
odd package contained Shaw' notebooks.

From a sitting position, Junior Ray, as though thrusting his bold hand into
the jaws and uncertain darkness of a sleeping catfish, reached and grabbed and
tossed, one by one, each of the notebooks at my feet until the heap stood at the
height of my knees.

The notebooks themselves were not actually notebooks: they were ledgers, a
plentiful supply of which had been available to Shaw in the almost empty and
long-unused plantation commissary that still stands even today in slow decay on
land once owned by Shaw's great-grandfather on his mother's side, Captain Pem-
berton Whitworth Ferry, a native of North Carolina, who had obtained land in
the Delta in the 1840s and had moved, at first, his family to Carrollton just up in
the Hills, then, later, after the Civil War, had moved them, finally, down into the
Delta's fertile alluvial jungle.

I picked up one of the ledgers, thought briefly of Thomas Wolfe, and opened
it to the first page. I quickly examined the contents of that page and that of several
more. A rapid survey of the pile confirmed my impression that every page of each
book was completely filled, back and front—in pencil. Shaw's handwriting was
atrocious but quite readable. And that was a great relief.]

I can see where it used to be,
though now, when I look,
it appears much like the exoskeleton
of a dead cicada.

And so the time and country that was pulled by beasts is gone, replaced by false weather, strange fields, and men with rubber skin.

All the mules, and horses too, are gone, burned in a fire at the edge of town, where constables stood on the road and shot at them and killed them with their Winchesters as they, both horse and mule, their manes, their flesh, their tails, all on fire, ran like living art, back and forth beneath the open shed and round and round, seeking haven in the safety of a burning barn.

I shall know my home by its indelible mark upon my longing, for it is the longing that is the plate on which the image is etched in distant light, where there are no angels, only the angelic.

There is no setting sun, only shadows for a time, and, then, it is that star again, whose light, itself, is shadow to all the rest, a screen to fool the eyes and hide the mystery, the distance, and the magnitude.

Surely in some land of pure form, the myth must still exist. I am not saying that it was good or that it was just or that it was right or that it was wrong. Myth has nothing to do with those things. Myth is, or was, and is what it is or was what it was. Unlike matter, It can be created, and destroyed.

The impossible is not attractive. Although, one can never

know whether anything is impossible. And that is exactly what
is attractive about Dostoyevsky's mouse: it is the intolerable
capacity to believe in infinite answers and unlimited options
without, necessarily, making assumptions. Certainly, if I had
been more the bullish "man of action" and less the mouse of
thought, I would have been a better soldier. But soldier I am,
and war this is. That I know. It is where that poses the problem.
Where is all this effort, all this drama, going on? I think I am in
Europe, the victim of a trick – the ambiguity here is acceptable
because both Europe and I have fallen for the same deception.
The question then becomes a matter of who is the trickster.
However, all of that is too much a digression, and I must deal
with the situation at hand, here and now, for it is I and not the
larger framework – which has no blood and has no bones –
that must live out my existence.

Still, just where is that? To be sure, there is nothing
humdrum about escape. And I have found the game to be not
one of escape and evasion so much as one of escape and
search, partly because evading these Nazis does not appear
very difficult, and that is why I am able to pursue my search,
as all the while they, poor Teutons, bumble about the landscape in search of me, sweating – no doubt even on these
clear, cold and brittle days that bathe the sleeping fields in
noisy ice – inside their rubber skins.

That is when cotton undershirts become the enemy.

You can do whatever you want to with the rest of that googah; I just don't want nobody to run off with it.

AND THEN THERE WAS that smart-ass black muthafukka, Bone
Face. That dumb sumbich spelt it like one word, *Boneface*, but
that's because, bein' black, he didn't know no better. 'Course,

he owned a lot of land and a whole buncha "cafes" all around the
county and especially in the back alley behind the stores in St.
Leo. And because of that, he pretty much controlled the rest of
the niggas, and that's why, when he died not too long ago, he
had the biggest funeral there ever was in St. Leo, and half the
people at it was white, the gotdamn sumbiches. If you didn't
know better, you'd think all them planters was a buncha Yan-
kee-ass nigga lovers. But they are a strange crew—probably
because so many of 'em goes up North to college. If it ain't that,
I don't know what it is. All I know is they ain't like good
Christian folks like it is back in Clay City. Hell, a planter don't
think he's alive unless he's drivin forty miles to go eat'n or
dancin', and he sho don't think it's Sunday unless he's got a
house full of niggas and a pitcher of martinis set'n beside his ass.
    Let me just clarifiy one other thing—them black
muthafukkas weren't no minority. Not in that little Delta
county, no-fukkin-sir. When I was deputy, back then, they was
twenty thousand people in the town and county combined, but
less than two thousand was white. And that's the way it was in
most of them Delta counties. That was back in the time when
the Fourth of July was still considered a day of mournin'. One
nem planters explained *that* to me one time. He said it was the
Fall of Vicksburg. I could see it. Although, if you want to know
the truth, that war didn't have nothin' to do with the likes of me
and my kind. I know I wouldna fought for them rich, slave-
ownin' muthafukkas. Plus, I sure as hell wouldna wanted no
slaves. Fuk that. The real slaves was the assholes who owned 'em,
if you want my opinion.
    Anyway, I guess because of my background it was hard for
me to ever *really* fit in down here in the Delta. But then, them
other white sumbiches wouldna fit in back where my people
come from in Clay City, over in the hills. And, actually, that has

a lot to do with what happened, once you know how to look at it.

It really could turn out that Voyd was the only one of 'em who truly saw my side of the thing. But, he's such a dumb sumbich, that don't say a lot for me. And I needed somebody to say somethin' for me, gotdamn it, even if I *was* on the wrong side. Here's what happened.

One day, about ten in the morning, Leland Shaw come into the office at the lumber company and told Miss Willy that he was goin' home. She said he didn't wait for no answer; he just turned around and walked out the door. Then, for several days nobody seen nothin' of him. But finally the neighbors realized he was inside his mama's house, and they got worried that he wasn't able to take care of hissef, whatever in the fuk that means, so they called Miss Helena Ferry, who was getting on up in years even then, and she called Dr. Austin, who was her cousin from Rosedale but who had set up practice in St. Leo back in the twenties, and he said leave it to him. So, the first thing he done was to call up Lawyer Montgomery, and him and Lawyer Montgomery went down to the bank and talked to the president, Mr. Humes. And since they was all three—or *four*, including Miss Helena—pretty much the same thing as family, they whipped up an idea that took care of the problem. For a moment.

They got Sheriff Holston and me to come over to the house and help 'em take Leland to the "Rest Wing" of the new hospital where they more or less fixed him up his own little apartment, which had a big pitcha-window lookin' east out across Highway 61 and an iron wreckin' bar across the door that opened into the main hall. For the time being, they said, they didn't want to send him up to Meffis to the Army hospital, nor did they want to ship him off to the insane asylum down at Whitfield. Lord, they said, that woulda been the end of him. Personally, I wished it hadda been. They said they believed Leland would be fine if he could just stay among people who knew him and that he would be happy, they believed, and *comfortable* there in the "Rest Wing" of the Mhoon County Hospital, right there in St. Leo, on the side of Highway 61. Truth is, they was all afraid he was gonna start runnin' around nekkid.

Well, boy, did those assholes have another thing comin'. They failed to realize that Leland Shaw didn't know who the fuk they was or give a shit about who cared about him or that he was suppose–ably in St. Leo "among people who knew him." As far as that crazy sumbich was concerned, he wuddn nowheres near St. Leo, and, in his warped-ass mind, all them kin and connections out there was probably the enemy. And, in my opinion, he wuddn about to be happy about nothin' until he could get back home—wherever in the fuk he may have thought that was.

ANOTHER THING I FORGOT to mention: he was real goosey. If you'd point your finger at him, he'd th'ow hissef on the floor and scramble around to get up under something. See, I figure that's because he believed them German soldiers was about to nail him. Same thing if anybody shined a light at him, he'd dive up under something. He was the craziest sumbich I ever saw. And how anybody could've wasted any time lookin' after him, I will never understand. I'da throwed his ass in the river a long time ago. People thought I was hard, but I say you had to be there. I know: *they* was there, too, but fukkum.

One night, the nurse shined a flashlight on him just to make sure he was in his bed asleep, and he leapt up like some kinda gotdamn animal and zipped off into a corner where she couldn't see him no more, but she knew he was in there and couldn't get out so she went on back down the hall and didn't say nothin' about it. But he musta been going through one of them real intense spells of believin' them German soldiers was comin' up on him, because the next day, which was the day after Christmas, 1958, he jumped through that pitcha-window at the cracker-dawn and run like a muthafukka. The nurse said she heard a crash, but had thought it was something out on the highway. The truth is she was asleep and didn't want that to come out.

Now, there it was, colder than the I-R-S, and that dicklicker skips off in nothin' but a pair of cotton khakis, some wool socks, brogan shoes, a flannel shirt from the Golden Rule, an olivedrab GI sweater, the kind that has buttons runnin' from the breastbone to the neck, one nem knit caps from the army surplus, and his daddy's old wine-colored heavy wool bathrobe, which was damn near too big for him but, I grant you, woulda provided him with a good deal of warmth. Oh, yeah, and a pair of blue mittens that had "Joy to the World" wrote all over 'em, which somebody from the Episcopal church had made and sent over to him for a Christmas present. And except for them mittens, that's what he wore every year when the weather turned cool. I guess it was his uniform.

The ground was so frozen he didn't leave no tracks, although somebody found a couple of PayDay candy–bar wrappers behind the Boll and Bloom Cafe out on the highway across from the lot that had all them scaly-bark trees, where the old Boy Sprout hut used to be.

Naturally, at first, the talk was that he hitched a ride to Meffis. But I said then, and I say now, no fool in his right mind woulda given a lift to a crazy lookin' sumbich like Leland Shaw was, dressed up in that big-ass bathrobe. So I never did believe he left the area. It turned out I was right, too, but all that come out little by little as time went by.

WELL, I NEVER SAW such a gotdamn commotion in all my life. The Boll and Bloom became the headquarters for the *volunteers* who wanted to help search for that crazy muthafukka. It was a good place to have a headquarters because that's where most of them volunteers was ever'day anyhow, even when they wuddn searchin' for nothin'.

I enjoyed the whole thing. Shoot, the highway patrol got in on it, and a group or two from out of town came up to help— well, after a while they was reports of a wild-ass lookin' sumbich showin' up here and there in about four or five counties around the Delta. That, in itself, didn't mean a whole lot because, if you ast me, the Delta had more wild-actin', weird-looking coksukkas than it could keep track of anyhow. Most of the reports turned out to be something else or nothin' at all, but one or two had some truth in 'em. Like the one from out there in the eastern part of the county around Dooley Spur, and another from over 'cross the levee in the bar' pits south of Mhoon's Landing. There were others that Voyd and I and sometimes some of the volunteers investigated, but we couldn't turn up nothin'. And the strange thing about it was that he was right up under our nose the whole fukkin time.

As I say, at first I wanted to save him and make ever'body happy; then, later, I wanted to kill him—and *also* make ever'body happy . . . but, as the thing drug on, I ceased to give a fuk about ever'body, and I just wanted to shoot his ass.

By that time it wouldn't have mattered who it was, but, you might say, he had become the most convenient target of what you also might say was a once-in-a-lifetime opportunity. And I sure as sheepshit wuddn gonna turn it down.

> I am a soldier of misfortune,
> though, even so, not an unhappy one. Indeed,

I speed by night on feet of light
to all the corners of this alien land,
where I am blocked and cannot proceed
for lack of stars
and high water.

I fly on foot with flashing talaria,
my body wrapped in the wool of a supplicant,
but my aim is armed in archetypes;
and, moving fast through the clear,
cold moonless night,
I am a particle of all the cosmic dust
within that bright galactic swipe above me, that, frankly,
warms my heart with its myriad, radiant islands
of atomic fire.

Pinpoints find me, fuel my velocity – I do not tire – I have
no schedule, and, as prey, I have but three concerns: escape,
evasion, and return.
But I cannot return
unless I know where I've gone,
and that is the relentless difficulty
which neither preachers
nor geographers can remedy.

A PLANTER DOWN NEAR TUTWILER said he saw a strange-actin,
funny-dressed feller runnin' around his equipment shed. Two
teenagers said they looked out of their car up on the levee and
seen a maniac with a hook for a hand. I'd like to know who told
that one for the first time. How many hook-handed maniacs
you reckon there could be? And why is it always teenagers who
sees 'em?

Anyhow, the point is that finally they was sightings of "the maniac" up and down Highway 61 as far south as Shelby and as far north as Dead Nigga Slough, up between Lake Cormorant and Walls. And it was when he began to be referred to as a maniac that started me to thinking about being able to blow him away and not having to explain it.

Now, if that sumbich had been the kinda good ol' boy I have some repect for, I'da had a whole different attitude about the entire episode. But he wuddn. He wuddn the kinda guy that a person growed up with and went out with after the ballgame on Fridays and screwed sheep with just for the hell of it. Screwin' sheep was supposed to be against the law, but what was they gon' do—put one nem little wooly muthafukkas on the witness stand? It'd a been my word against hers anyhow.

They used to say that down at State College they was a half-human, half-sheep thing in a jar. It sounded pretty awful, mainly because of what it meant might happen to you if you wuddn careful. Think about it. It would be *the* unde-fukkin-niable proof that you'd been out screwin' sheep. I mean, don't you know back then they was a lotta good ol' boys down there at Cow College that hated to look at that thing in the jar on account of they was afraid they was gonna see their spit'n image.

Some people, especially women, find it hard to believe all that went on, but it did, and for as far back as I can remember, too, till finally they wuddn no more livestock due to the way the farmin' situation changed and all. But, hell, by then it didn't make no difference no way, 'cause I was already long growed up and didn't care about that kinda thing no more. But I'll tell you what, every time I'm somewheres of a Sunday, which ain't much, and they're servin' lamb and mint jelly, I always feel a little bit uneasy. It's things like that, later on, that make you think about what you're going to do before you do it instead of just shoot'n from the hip, if you know what I mean. I guess if I could say one thing about screwin' sheep, it really made me appreciate family values.

But it was a lotta fun. We had us a time back in nem days. They was this one ewe that belonged to old man Peyton, and we used to go out and catch her in his pasture out near the levee. One night that old ewe looked back over her shoulder at me and said, "Junior Ray, you're a baaaaaad boy."

That's a joke.

Why is it men are the only ones that do shit like that? I mean, can't you just see a whole carload of cheerleaders flingin' empty pints of Jim Beam out the windows, tearin' out along a gravel road to fuk sheep? Or, better yet, after the big game, one of the high school heroes says to his girlfriend, "Want to go to the dance?" and she says, "Hell, no, muthafukka, I wanta go screw sheep." That could be that sumbich's greatest nightmare, and it's no wonder them planters was in such a sweat to get mechanized and stick to row crops.

> But there were mules,
> and mules were food
> and numerous enough
> to fatten the vultures who,
>   at that very moment, may, in fact, have been consuming
> the time and place, devouring it hunk by hunk until, finally,
> only the bones remain and those so scattered only mice can
> find them.

ANYHOW, GET'N BACK to what I was tellin you, one day in the middle of all that commotion over the disappearance of that asshole Leland Shaw, I was set'n in the Sheriff's office with my feet up on my desk, eat'n one nem pimento cheese sammidges

the Methodist ladies sent over, and drinkin' a Coke, and I
looked over at Voyd who was read'n last month's *Field and
Stream*, and I said, "Voyd," and he didn't say nothin', and I said,
"Voyd, I'mo find that gotdamn maniac." And Voyd, still
readin' *Field and Stream*—or more likely just lookin' at the
pitchers—says, "Junior Ray, that sumbich ain't no maniac."

And I said, "Well, he's sure as shit gon' be one when I get
through with his ass—I'mo find that sumbich—I'mo find 'im!"

"You not gon' do doodly squat, Junior Ray," he says to me.
"You couldn't find your dick with a hard on, much less some
crazy fool runnin' around the county scarin' one half of ever'body
to death and worryin' the shit out of the other half about
whether he's gon' catch cold or not."

"Well, Voyd," I said, "You're right about one thing—*I* ain't
gonna find him—*we* are gonna find him, and *we* are gon' get
started right now, so get your ass up and come on!"

We went out the side door of the courthouse, got in my
patrol car, which was parked under the big white oak, and
scratched off outa the parking lot. I turned on the blue lights and
the sireen, and took off out the Beat Line Road toward Savage
and the Yellow Dog.

Just about all the roads was still gravel then, except for
Highway 61; so, dry as it was, I raised a lotta dust blastin' outta
town on the Beat Line Road, goin' east. Then I cut off the blue
lights and the sireen when we got past the city dump. We was
gonna go check out a so-called sighting by some niggas out
between Savage and Prichard. One of 'em said he heard a
painter, and the other two said it was a man howlin' out in the
woods over on the other side of the Yellow Dog, between the
railroad tracks and the Coldwater River.

I didn't believe it was no *painters* left around there, but
Voyd claimed Leroy Whalum swore they was one right out

where we was goin' and said *Leroy said* he'd heard it and seen its footprints in a rice field as far up as Lost Lake.

Anyhow, when me and Voyd was clippin' along out the Beat Line road, just fo we got to the Dog, Voyd says, "looky yonder at that old silo." And I says, "Uhn-huhn," not thinkin' much about it. And Voyd says, "That sumbich is full of cotton seeds." Now that got my attention, for a moment anyway, and I said, "That's a gotdamnn helluva thing to have in a silo. Who put cotton seeds in it?" And Voyd said he didn't know but that, one afternoon, him and Sunflow'r was parked out there the other side of it, and he got out of the car to take a leak and decided to look up in the chute. And that's when he found out the thing was jam-ass-packed to the top with old cotton seeds, and they wasn't no tellin' how long they'd been there.

Now, the silo itsef, which was a big, tall muthafukka, had been put there in about 1914, and I knew that because, at the Rotary Club one day when I was the guest of Sheriff Holston, Judge Lowe had made a talk on the history of the county, and he pointed out that that silo had been built way back then by a buncha Yankees from up in Wisconsin who rented the land from old Miss Helena Ferry's father and wanted to raise milk cows on the property, but that didn't last long, with the mosquitos and the heat and the damp-ass weather—but them Yankees always was a silly-ass lot . . . anyway, finally, the Wisconsin outfit gave it up, and Miss Helena rented it out for row crops. I don't know who farmed it, but, at some point, somebody filled that thing full of cotton seeds and just left them there.

> I look now across the clear, cold light
> of this winter plain
> and see the marsh hawk gliding low,

just above the sedge,
along the ditch.
No doubt rabbits are trembling
beneath the swift shadow of this early harrier,
hungry, borne up not by air
but by beauty.

In the distance the patrol approaches at port arms, in a line of skirmishers, Teutonic, in search of Celts. Their eyes burn with murder. Their pace is deliberate and unceasing. Yet, it is I who have found them and not the reverse, and they are the sign that I am not at home. I do not share their fondness for kartoffels.

3

The Silo — The Search for Shaw — The Hopping Man — Niggas & Planters — Miss Helena Ferry — Disappearing Footprints — Mr. X and the Light-Skinned Miss Atlanta Birmingham Jackson

But, see, I missed the barn door. That silo, fulla them cotton seeds, was where that crazy muthafukka Leland Shaw had holed up and was hiding probably right then and there when Voyd and me was ridin' along lookin' at the thing. Voyd, he's the kinda sumbich that just says whatever pops into his eyeballs. His mouth is just sort of a safety valve to let the air out of his head. But I can't be too proud mysef, since I didn't see the obvious when the answer to the question of where Leland was came out of Voyd's mouth. Well, he didn't make the connection neither; and then, too, we didn't have any idea at the time what direction the sumbich had gone in.

But that silo was where it turned out he had been hiding all along, and it was that silo in particular that made it possible for him to survive that long a time in the middle of the winter like that, 'cause it was colder than shit. I'm talking about whole weeks of those cold, cold clear days when there was ice all over the ground, and the temperature didn't never get no higher than thirty-two. Now, that may be fine for some asshole in Alaska that lives in a' igloo, but for the average person in the Mississippi Delta, it is fukkin brutal. So don't you see, set'n up in there, burrowed down on top of that tower of old cotton seeds, Leland Shaw coulda slept like a baby in his birthday suit and still been just as warm as a doodle bug. It almost wouldna mattered how cold it was. Plus, bein' up so high off the ground and the Delta being so fukkin flat, he could see out all over the place for a long ways around.

Plain as it was, I didn't put it together at the time. I guess I thought possibly he was hol'n up in one nem empty nigga houses still set'n out in the fields. By now most of them old abandoned shacks have been dozed down or else it's so growed up around 'em it just looks like a thicket, and you can't tell it was never no house there, covered up with all them vines and bushes and willow trees. 'Course I know a planter, up around Walls, who says that no matter what you do or however many times you plow over it, you can't never get rid of a house site.

I *would* say they was *all* nigga houses, but, the truth is, I can't—they's exactly like the kind my daddy and mama and me and my brothers lived in when we first come down to the Delta. And we was white people. We was sharecroppers and we worked a little piece of land out on the east side of the highway, near the Coldwater River, in the Delta but right at the edge of it near the foot of the hills. Tell you how bad off we was, a buncha times in the winter the fukkin snow would fly in through the planks on the wall, and I don't even want to talk about the roof—but, bad off as we was, we never did piss through the floor boards like ol' Miz Dundrum and that dumbfukkin daughter of hers who, the both of 'em, would screw them carloads of town boys for a quarter a throw. I guess, when you come to think of it, maybe those two silly things didn't have no choice, both of 'em bein' so po-ass, and ignorant. Hell, maybe they was just lucky as shit, because I sure as hell don't know why any sumbich in his right mind would want to fuk 'em. Shit, they didn't *never* take no bath. 'Specially in the winter. Hotdamn, I wouldna fukked that with a broomstick. Well, they never went nowhere, so I don't guess it made much difference.

That's why, lemme tell you, I'm glad there ain't no more hand labor 'cause that means there ain't *no* chance in hell I'd ever have to work in a cotton field again. Jee-zuss Christ, when I wuddn no more than in the third grade, I had worked a whole two weeks pickin' cotton just so I could buy an old flannel shirt to wear to school, and some gotdamn candy-ass town boy tore it when we was out on the playground—well, I have to say he didn't do it on purpose, I know that now, but, fukkim, I beat the livin' shit out of him anyway, and that muthafukka remembers it to this very cotton-fukkin-pickin day. The funny thing is, I truly think he still feels kinda bad about tearin' the shirt.

Get'n that deputy job changed a lotta things for me—and for my mama and daddy and nem, too. Hell, some folks think I'm kidd'n, but I guarantee you there ain't a day goes by that I don't say, "Thank you, Jesus! Thank *you* . . . for them fukkin cotton pickin' machines!"

ANYHOW, VOYD AND ME went on out toward Savage and Prichard. We interviewed a half dozen or so niggas living out there who claimed they had either seen or heard what they said was a crazy man runnin' around out in the woods east of the Yellow Dog. However, two of 'em flat out stated what they heard was a *painter*. They said they had heard and seen *painters* one or two times before in them woods, and I come around to sayin' I guess I could believe it because them woods wuddn no joke, not by a longshot. In nem days it was just as easy to get lost out there as it was over 'cross the levee. And, too, I bore in mind that Voyd had said that Leroy Whalum claimed one—a *painter*—come through out there all the time since he was a boy; and, frankly, I wouldna never had no reason to doubt Leroy. Hell, he taught me all I know about how to use a slapjack. He was a constable back then, when he was alive, and he used to be the one we put downtown on Sad'dy to keep the niggas in line.

After we had done heard enough, me and Voyd took a loggin' road that went way back in the woods. It was dry as a bone and colder than a popsicle, so we didn't have no trouble drivin' back in there in the patrol car. After a while we stopped drivin' and got out of the car and started walkin'. But it was get'n dark. That's when most of the howlin' had been goin' on, according to the reports. Me and Voyd kept to the log road and walked deeper into the woods. It was pitch-ass black, and silent as an hootie owl comin' in on a rabbit. Cold as it was, it seemed like the onliest thing rustlin' around makin' any noise at all was Voyd and me.

Pretty soon we come to an open place, and it's still darker than ditchwater, and Voyd says, "Let's go back to the car." And I said, "Aw-ight. Let's go. I don't think we're gonna find nothin' out here tonight. I'm freezin' my ass off." And then Voyd says, "Hold on. You hear that?"

"Hear what?" I said, 'cause I didn't hear nothin'.

"That," he said again, and then I heard it. It sounded like somebody snikkerin'. Man, my fukkin hair stood up. We started th'owin them flashlight beams ever' whicha way, but we couldn't see what it was. Then, there it come again, ever so softly, kind of a giggle, off in the dark, but real close. I mean, son, if something is gonna get your ass, I don't much want it to be fukkin invisible and laughin' at the same time. Hell, I think I could stand to hear a growl or a howl or a roar of some kind

before I'd want to deal with a thing out there in the dark kinda
snikkering and gigglin' soft like that, like a fukkin weird-ass
some-kinda-girl monster. I mean, I don't know how the hell to
describe it, except to say that it made my asshole slam shut.

"That ain't no *painter*," Voyd said. And all the time, this
thing is out there in the dark, gigglin' and snikkerin', and
beginning to hum a little bit; then it started singing—real soft—
la la la, and then it changed over to sa sa sa, and we still could not
spot whatever it was with our lights—oh, we could hear it
movin' around, and we knew what direction it was in, but we
could not locate it with the lights.

"Voyd," I said, "let's get the fuk outta here." But that little
chicken-ass sumbich was already cut'n a trail back down the log
road. "Wait on me, you sunavabitch!" I hollered, but that fukka
was disappearin' around a bend, leavin' my ass back there all
alone with that gotdamn hummin' thing, which had gone silent,
and that was even worse. Then, just as I was about to light out
behind him, here come him and his flashlight be-boppin' up
and down back around the bend toward me. "What the fuk?" I
thought. I knew he wuddn comin' back because I had hollered
after him. He was comin' back because somethin' was chasin' his
ass.

"Junior Ray!" he hollered. "Junior Ray! — Junior Ray! —
Junior Ray! — Shoot this thing! Don't let it get me!" Voyd was
yip-yappin' like one nem little what I calls "punt" dogs—I
named 'em that because they ain't much more'n a lil' ol' bitty
nervous ball of hair and a big-ass mouth, and I could just take
my foot and "punt" 'em across the room. Anyway, I was
beginnin' to think we was in some kinda weird fukkin movie. I
couldn' see nothin' behind him, and the whole thing was about
to turn my blood to fukkin Double-Cola. Plus, he was just
about *babblin'* now and near 'bout knocked me down. I didn't

know what the fuk was goin' on. Then, I heard it. They was a whole lot of commotion comin' up behind him, and it was that gigglin' thing, and it was cacklin' pretty loud and start'n to holler itsef, which, by that time, was what all three of us was doin'.

I never seen nothin' like it. I th'owd up my flashlight, and there not five feet in front of me was the gotdamndest thang I ever laid my eyes on. Screechin' and laughin' and jumpin' up and down three or four feet, it looked like, off the ground, like he was on a pogo stick, was the wildest looking muthafukka I ever saw. I damn near passed out. I mean you just don't expect nothin' like that in your whole fukkin life.

So there we was. This wild muthafukka was jumpin', and we was jumpin'. He was hollerin', and we was hollerin'. And nobody was goin' nowhere. We was just all three hoppin' up and down hollerin' in the woods in the middle of the night. I'm damn glad they wuddn no coon hunters out there 'cause Voyd and I would have been the laughin' stock of Mhoon County if it had ever got back. But we was fortunate the sumbich was so fukkin crazy 'cause he never said nothin' about how we acted— hell, he probably thought it was normal. Anyway, without warnin' he stops, stands dead still, and looks at Voyd and me and says: "Do you gentleman accept the Lord Jesus Christ as your personal savior?" And Voyd and me, both, at the same time, said: "Fuk yeah." "A-fukkin-men," said Voyd. Both of us was frozen thinkin' he was gonna start boundin' up and down again, and he was big, too. I don't think Voyd and I coulda handled him if things hadn't turned out the way they did. Oh, yeah, he was a white man, too. At first I couldn tell, and I thought he had to be a nigga, but then I said to myself, "No fukkin nigga would be out here in the middle of the gotdamn woods in the middle of the winter and especially in the dark."

Those sumbiches hate all three of them things. So I knew only a white man would be crazy enough to be that crazy. And it was.

"Are you a preacher?" I ast him.

"Yes, son, I am," he said.

"Well," I said, "if you don't mind me askin', what are you doin' out here in the woods?"

"I am searching for Mary and Joseph and the Christ Child," he said. "Have you seen them?"

"Yeah," I said. "We seen 'em, and we can show you where they're at." Then I got a little worried because he seemed to get somewhat agitated, and I was sure he was gonna go off and start hollerin' and hoppin' again, because he come out in a loud voice and said, "There is no room at the inn!"

But Voyd piped up and said, "Yes it is, too! They's *plenty* of room at the inn, and we're goin' there now."

"Yeah," I said, "we're on our way to the inn right this fukkin minute. You want to come along?" And he started to hop ever so slightly and started grinnin and shakin' his head to indicate he did, and I said to him, "Behold the light, brother. Follow the light, and it'll take us to the inn."

"And to the *truth!*" Voyd piped up, 'cause he was get'n into it, too, and we was on a roll.

Well, that sumbich stayed right in the spot of the flashlight wherever I put it. No matter whether I th'owed it on the road ahead of us or off in the bushes, he stayed right in the light, and I could make him go thisaway or thataway like one nem little toy cars. I coulda pointed it up a tree, and that sumbich woulda clumb right up it—he'd find the spot and try to stay right smack in the middle of it and go wherever I wanted him to, just like he was on the end of a stick or somethin, and so there we went, with me shinin' the light and him hoppin' and singin' and hummin' and even let'n out a little holler ever' now and then all the way back to the patrol car; and Voyd run and opened the back door, and I shined the light up inside the vehicle, and the crazy preacher just hopped and bopped right on into the back seat, and I give the light to Voyd who got in the back seat beside him so's we could keep it shinin' down on his feet thinkin' he would sit still and not try to get out, and we hauled him on in to St. Leo and put him in jail.

Even though that sumbich smelled something awful and Voyd and me was gaggin' by the time we got him to the jailhouse, the truth is, I kinda got to like him. I don't know why unless it had somethin' to do with how easy he was to manage with the flashlight. It was fukkin unreal. I wouldna never believed a little thing like light coulda done all that. Plus, it turned out he, the crazy hoppin' man, was the brother of a rough sumbich who lived up between Prichard and Arkabutla who stayed drunk all the time and, so he claimed, didn't even know, one, that his brother was that crazy or, two, that he'd gone off down in the bottoms, hoppin' and howlin' back in the woods.

Sheriff Holston and the state handled it from there. I was glad, too, 'cause I'd had about a-fukkin-nuff. And, that next morning, Miss Florence, who ran the Sheriff's office, said, "Well, Junior Ray, I see you and Voyd found yoursefs a maniac." And I said, "Yes'm, but he wuddn the one we was lookin' for."

> Further, it is not fair of me to say that the inhabitants here are Germans. Frankly, I do not know who they are or what they are, owing to their habit of wearing rubber skin.

SOMETIMES I JUST DON'T KNOW who I hated the worst, niggas or planters. Back in nem days there wuddn a helluva lot of difference between the two. All them planters was kin and connected, and all them niggas was kin and connected; and, if you ast me, all them niggas and planters was kin and connected with each other if you really thought about it and saw how many of 'em damn near looked alike. Back then, all the niggas was supposed to belong to the planters—a three thousand-acre place mighta easily had a hunnerd and seventy-five *families* living on it and all of 'em niggas, which, to my mind, made it seem like more sense to say them planters belonged to the niggas. Hell, they couldna been planters without 'em. Back then a planter couldn't chew his gotdamn food without a nigga standin' right there by him. Niggas did everything. Them planters never did shit. They wanted the niggas to do ever'thing for 'em except fuck their wives, and for all I know they mighta done that too. It wuddn that them planters was lazy; it's just that, like the niggas, they didn't know no other way. And that's the way it was. Plus, they treated people like me like some kinda gotdamn varmit; yet, they treated the niggas just like they was actual human beings, and that's because most of them planters had done growed up with 'em ever since they was chirren. I never did understand it, mysef. Well, a lotta things was different . . . back in nem days.

But, even though I hated the *en*tire lot of 'em, I couldn't let on that I did. I never had no choice. I was at the total gotdamn mercy of all them coksukkin niggas and planters. I mean, hell, it seemed like everybody was kin to *ever*'body except me, down here in the Delta. 'Course, I had relatives back in Clay City, who I did'n give a shit about, but that ain't the Delta. That's in the hills. It's a big difference. I know people find this hard to believe, but Mississippi wuddn just one kinda state. It was more like about three, if you include the Coast and all them fukkin Catholics.

Of course, the larger implications include the fact that with each tick and tock, a certain amount of the sun is exhausted, and, drop by drop, molecule by molecule, the thing is on its way out. Not that I would let a dying fireball stand in my path, but I do believe one ought to recognize the irreversible nature of reality, particularly if one wants to avoid it.

NOW, ABOUT ALL THAT "who's kin to who" shit: here's what made it a serious matter back when I was a deputy tryin' to find out where that crazy Leland Shaw run off to. Well, that's a nice way to put it, when what I was aimin' to do was to murder his ass and have some fun in the process. Anyway, first, there was Miss Helena Ferry and her brother, "Sticks." He got that name because he was so fukkin skinny. Plus, he was a worthless, drunk-ass, smart-mouth sunavabitch, and I'm glad he's dead. And he didn't have a whole lot to do with the Leland Shaw thing anyway, but Miss Helena did. They was the brother and sister of Leland Shaw's mama. They was planters—or put it this way, they was part of that buncha sumbiches.

I said "Sticks" Ferry didn't have much to do with the episode, but that depends on how you look it. You see, he, it was widely known, was the father of that high-yellow bitch who come back down here that time with all the Mohammedan muthafukkas. Her name was Atlanta Birmingham Jackson, and she grew up right down there in St. Leo, well, up north of it in what they called the Sub, which was short for subdivision, which it definitely was not, in the usual sense. So, that made her and her light-skinned ass the actual first cousin of Leland Shaw, although nobody was supposed to mention it. *Her* mama was damn near white to begin with. And, her grandmama had worked for the Ferrys. She had been the nurse for Miss Helena and Sticks and the rest of 'em, so they say. I'd hate to think whose child *she* was. But this just proves what I was sayin' a while ago. Anyhow, I don't give a shit about none of that except in so far as how it explains the tie-in and what it had to do with the whole fukkin thing and why I never got to unload that thirty-eight I toted—and still do—on Leland Shaw.

So, there was that high-yellow bitch. Then there was the Mohammedans. They was called the Fruit, and they worked for Mr. X who lived in Chicago, and the high-yellow bitch was his girl-friend. The Fruit never said nothing, they just pissed me off. And they drove around in this big-ass Cadillac limousine with windows you couldn't see nothing through. That was the first time I ever saw them kinda windows, and that was way back yonder.

In addition to the high-yellow bitch and the Fruit, there was Bone Face, all his crew, and another black bastud by the name of Milton Casequarter who had a store midway between St. Leo and Dooley out the Beat Line Road where you turn off to go to Walnut Lake, which ain't no more a lake than I am.

All them was niggas.

Now, here was the situation: Leland Shaw run off. Nobody knowed where he was. Lots of reports came in about a maniac runnin' all over the place between Lake Cormorant and Shelby, up and down Highway 61, mostly the northwest part of the Delta, though we was get'n some sightings from over as far as Tutwiler and Lambert. But, all the time, that sumbich never left Mhoon County and was hid'n in a silo—which, as I said a while ago, was full of old cotton seeds.

Through the years I have pieced this thing together to try to understand why I couldn't have worked it out no better than I did. Lord fukkin knows I tried.

I ast myself—what was he eat'n? If a sumbich is out there somewhere hide'n in the bushes or whatever, what was he livin' on? I couldn't figure it out. Now, of course, *now,* I know how he did it. He had help and plenty of it. And the funny part about that is I don't think he even knew he was being helped. I guarantee you that crazy fukka thought he was managin' it all on his crazy-ass own, livin' off the fukkin land.

But he was get'n his food from Milton Casequarter's store. Shaw went out at night, mostly. It was colder'n shit, but he would walk like a muthafukka, wrapped up in that big wool bathrobe, and he would knock off about four miles an hour; apparently he did not know what tired was, bein' so fukkin crazy. Anyhow, within the first two or three nights, he come back by Casequarter's store, maybe around four-o-clock in the morning, and he discovers the truck from the wholesale has left a buncha stuff on the porch of the store, candy bars, bread, cold drinks, and them real red weenies all strung together, like you seen in all them country stores back in nem days. Casequarter had an old un-plugged freezer on the porch that he used in the winter to keep the cold-drinks and the milk and bread and other stuff from freezin' when the wholesale truck left the stuff on the porch of the store. The truckdriver would put the things that ought not to freeze in the freezer, and Casequarter would transfer it inside after he opened up the store around seven-thirty.

Shaw found all that, and looked inside the freezer, and he was set. Well, he stole it the first few nights, then Casequarter saw him, realized why his orders had been short, and started makin' up little packets in sacks and put'n 'em out on the bench and in the freezer, so Shaw could find 'em and not have as much trouble carry'n 'em off. It was them coksukkin sacks and candy bar wrappers that eventually told me he was up in that silo.

'Course, it's easy to go backwards now and see it all so clearly. Back then it was a different story. I didn't piece it together until it was over. Well, fuk, I was doin' it all near 'bout on my own, except for when Voyd was with me, and that ain't sayin' much.

So that's how he was eat'n. He'd sleep all day, and he'd walk like a muthafukka all night. Hell, in six hours, he could cover a lot of territory, and he didn't always come back that same night to the silo, if he found a place by morning he could sleep and be warm in.

And all the time, I was after him—even when all the reports about a maniac had stopped coming in and people had gotten interested in other things, I was still after him.

WELL, IT *WAS* CRAZY. Most people seemed to want him found, and a buncha others seemed like they did not want him found— by me, anyway—and I think that is what the whole thing was about, finally. Fukkum. They mighta all wanted him to be somewhere else, safe and where they could put their finger on him, but they didn't want *me* to be the one who found the muthafukka, 'cause they knew I'd kill him.

It was complicated. First, every swingin' dick in the county and up and down Highway 61 was lookin' for him. Then, finally, that narrowed down to just a few who really cared about him in some way or another, chief of which was his loony old aunt, Miss Helena Ferry. Here's what happened.

One day Bone Face sent Miss Helena word that some of his "rabbit hunters" had spied "Mister Leland" out in her field where the silo was. Bone Face told her they knew he was hide'n out in the silo, and Bone Face further added that it was a warm place because "it ain't fulla nothin' but good ol' cotton seeds all the way to the top." So Miss Helena calls him over, but, in the meantime, Milton Casequarter shows up at Miss Helena's back porch and says he don't know where "Mister Leland" is but that he has been providing food for him for a few days and will continue to do so, if that is all right with Miss Helena. Miss Helena told him it was and for him to send her the bill for the food. He said "Yas'm," but I happen to know he never did—not because he was so much on the side of Shaw as it was he was against me personally; although I do understand that old Mr. Ferry, Miss Helena's father, had helped him get started in bizness and did not take advantage of him, like I sure as shit would have if it had'a been me.

Miss Helena, then, meets with Bone Face, and they drink coffee in her kitchen. He sits there with the bill of his cap pulled down on the side of his head because he liked to look as though he was just another ignorant-ass field hand shufflin' his feet and sayin' yassuh, when all the fukkin time he really is, no matter what I say, smarter than a whole coksukkin carload of foxes plus bein' one of the richest muthafukkas in the county. His hobby was driving around old cars that looked like they was all broke down, but when somebody would pull up alongside him on Highway 61 , he'd blast away like a fukkin rocketship 'cause under the hood he had a specially made customized motor put in there for him up in De-Troit. He was a gotdamn piece of work, and he controlled near 'bout all the niggas for a long way around, all except Milton Casequarter, Henry Lion (who was a half-Jew nigga undertaker), the school teachers, and a few others, but they didn't need his kind of controllin' anyway. All the rest who drank his whiskey, threw his dice, and fukked his whores needed somebody to keep 'em in line when the nigga school teachers, Milton Casequarter, and even that slick-ass Henry Lion stirred up 'em up and tried to get 'em to vote.

That was the one dog that definitely was not gon' hunt back in nem days. The niggas could do just about anything you—or they—could think of, includin' murder, but they could not vote and better not fukkin try it. A few was always allowed to cast a ballot—I'm talking about maybe a half a dozen, but that was it—and, because they was Republicans, they couldn't never vote in the primary, because Miss'ssippi was a one-party state in them days, and that was the Democrats. Now it's all fukkin flip-flopped and the white peoples is the Republicans. I can't keep up with that shit.

Anyhow. Miss Helena tells Bone Face what Milton Casequarter had told her about the food, and Bone Face allowed he already knew it and had his "rabbit hunters" keepin' an eye on her nephew . . . and, I found out, on me, too.

And he told her two other things. He said that sometimes "Mister Leland's tracks disappears." Well, some fukkin times there weren't no tracks even in the mud because it was all froze over, but what he meant was that when there was tracks across't a field, sometimes they just stopped, and the niggas followin' 'em couldn't figure out what was goin' on. And I ain't sayin' I could have either. It kinda makes your skin crawl.

Let's get one thing straight: I ain't sayin' all niggas is dumber'n shit. I wish to hell I *could* say it, but it's just that they have a funny way of thinkin' about things that is different from the way a white man thinks. It's like they always come at a thing from some un-fukkin-imaginable direction, but that's probably because they've *always* been on the wrong end of just damn near ever'thing, and so, I guess, they can just naturally see almost anything in a way nobody else ever could.

Anyway, fukkum. I used to swear I was gonna move to Alabama where there weren't no niggas, but I guess even I kinda got used to 'em after a while. And if I did move to one of them other places, over towards Cullman, I'd be mighty hard up to find somebody to hate. And that'd be a gotdamn tragedy. So screw it—I'm happy where I am.

Now the second other thing he told Miss Helena was that Atlanta Birmingham Jackson was back in town and was looking for a piece of land to buy for Mr. X, the boss of them Mohammedan muthafukkas up in Chicago, or one of 'em anyway. It was not clear what he wanted to do with it, but it was clear that he wanted to own some. Bone Face brung Miss Helena up to date by telling her that Atlanta, the high-yellow bitch I've been talkin' about, had been for many fukkin years the woman of Mr. X, or one of 'em anyway, and that she had done well financially. He also told Miss Helena that Miss-fukkin-Jackson was traveling around in a long-ass black Cadillac limousine with four big black bucks which, as I have mentioned, were known as the Fruit and that they had been sent down by Mr. X as her assistants, or some such shit, but more likely to keep an eye on her high-yellow ass.

Miss Helena allowed she had seen that automobile rollin' around town but that she couldn't see inside it. Bone Face said it was nothin' to worry about, they was just lookin' and wuddn nothin' goin' on. All they was interested in was buying a piece of land.

The light bulb musta gone on over Miss Helena's head, because she asked Bone Face to tell Atlanta Birmingham Jackson to come see her. You realize, of course, the high-yellow bitch was actually her fukkin niece—which neither she nor the high-yellow bitch would ever come right out and acknowledge—well, they didn't have to because, besides lookin' alike, they both knew it anyhow. It was one of them weird-ass understood things between planters and niggas *I never understood.*

The long and the short of it is this. Miss Helena and Atlanta Birmingham Jackson had coffee, too, but up in the livin' room and served to 'em by Queenasheba, Miss Helena's maid, while the Fruit sat outside in the car and waited. The house, which is gone now, was right in the middle of town, on a corner, with a big side yard that took up about a third of the whole block. It sat nearly smack-ass on the street and had a sidewalk, a big cotton-wood, and a sweetgum tree in front of it, right at an intersection, and was across the street from, at that time, a long row of nigga houses which later was tore down so they could build a new Mississippi Power and Light office.

And it was also across the *other* street from the old telephone operators' office which was built way up off the ground so, I reckon, high water couldn't get into it and fuk up the phones. Later, when the dial system come in, they turned the phone office into a beauty parlor.

But here's what happened. Miss Helena makes a fukkin deal with the high-yellow bitch, who is her niece and therefore Leland Shaw's first cousin—because Atlanta's father was, apparently, Miss Helena's no-count brother, "Sticks" Ferry, who drank hissef to death. Well, at least the sumbich died doin' what he liked to do. And bein' no-count was his chosen profession. 'Course, down there in the Delta you could be no-count but still be a bigshot if you was born into it. And there wuddn a whole lot you could do that would change that, if you was part of them planters, unless you just got up and waved your dick around in church. But even then, whenever there was a wedding or a party, though they might not let you in the house, they'd still send you an invitation.

Anyhow, the deal was this. Miss Helena told Atlanta Birming-fukkin-ham Jackson that she didn't have to buy no land. She told her she would give her a hun'erd acres if she, Miss High Yellow, would agree to take Leland Shaw back to Chicago with them and look after him for the rest of his life. Miss Helena said, too, that even if they didn't agree to that, the land should go to Atlanta anyhow because it ought to be hers, since it amounted to her, Miss Helena's, brother's former share of a quarter section, and added that she felt Mister "Sticks," her brother, would want Atlanta to have it because he had been "so fond of your mother." However, the hard facts is that whether or not Atlanta had any right to it was beside the point because she flat-ass wuddn gonna get it unless she did agree to take care of Leland Shaw, if and when Bone Face's "helpers" could get hold of him before "that awful Junior Ray Loveblood did and something terrible happened." Miss Helena was tough as a mule steak when she wanted to be.

But Atlanta did agree. And the Fruit agreed, too. They believed *Aller* would bless their asses; at least that is what I heard Mr. X told them. It seems he thought he was was gonna get the deed to the property, but I heard Atlanta surprised the shit out of him and kept hold of it but said he could use it for the good of the movement any time he wanted to and that he was certainly welcome to the income from it, but that for sentimental reasons she had to keep the land "in the family" so to speak; and though he might not'a liked it, he couldn't do nothin' about it, and the idea of income appealed to him a whole helluva lot— for the good of the movement of-fukkin-course—and that way she kept hold of Mr. X *and* the land, too. Them Mohammedans never did do nothin' with it that I know of, and now it is rented out to one nem huge-ass farmin' operations at about ninety fukkin dollars an acre because it is that fine sandy kinda land that's good for cotton, and it has a hun'red acres of cotton base, which means Mr. X or, by this time, Miss High Yellow, gets nine-fukkin-thousand dollars a year off of it—Hell, he may be dead for all I know, and she may be too, but I doubt it. Fukkum.

And so there it was. Me against Miss Helena Ferry and her planter kin, Bone Face and all his nigga entertainment empire, Atlanta Birmingham Jackson with all her half-white planter blood, and them Mohammedan coksukkas—the Fruit—and, if you want to include him, that uppity black store-ownin' sunavabitch, Milton Casequarter. And all of us, the planters, the niggas, and me, was runnin' around chasin' after something nobody could pin down. Somehow, I couldn't help but think that was the way it had always been.

Well, I had to say all that so that everything else that Voyd and me did would make more sense. I had to lay out the situation as clear as I could.

I was up against a lot.

They are smart, these Germans, but there are some things they simply cannot catch on to. It's all a matter of detail – and, I grant you, Teutons are extremely attentive to detail, but subtlety escapes them. You must bop them over the kopf with a sausage. They cannot comprehend subtlety if it is smaller than a potato or has no bosoms in an iron brassiere.

4

Quicksand — More About Footprints —
The Nite Al Cafe & Club — Voyd
Goes Home Nekkid

I NEVER CAUGHT HIM, BUT I SEEN HIM. NOT ALL THE REPORTS we got was false—but there again, even when they was false, it's my belief people did see somethin'—just like when Voyd and me found the hoppin' man.

Bear in mind that sumbich could walk off twelve miles in three hours, which ain't nothin' when you're movin' fast on a cold day—or cold-ass night, whichever. Anyway, while all this was goin' on, Miss Florence come in to the County Clerk's office where I was shootin' the shit with the secretary and says, "Junior Ray, some Meffis people called in from the Cut-Off and said they saw what looked like a man dressed in a housecoat walking out on that levee spur that goes over toward Devil's Hole."

Voyd wuddn doin' nothin', as usual, except playin' dominoes at the City Barber Shop, so I stopped by there and picked him up, and we went out toward the Cut-Off, got on top of the levee and turned north in the direction of Mhoon's Landing. The spur was off to the left between where we come up on the levee and Mhoon's. Let me explain about the Cut-Off. It's an artificial oxbow lake made by the U.S. Army Corps of Engineers in 1942. They just got a buncha dynamite and blew off a big-ass loop in the river which had caused towboats to travel miles in a fukkin enormous bend and wind up not havin' gone but about two hunnerd yards or some such shit as that, so they just made a fukkin lake out of the loop, and it's called the Cut-Off. And it was then and is now a helluva a big attraction for people from Meffis who like to fish, plus a lot of 'em have little cabins out there, and now they's some who actually live there and drive in to Meffis every day during the week to work.

Back then it was still pretty wild out there in the woods across the levee. They was ever'thing from wild hogs to deer and turkeys, bobcats and coons, and no tellin' what else. Naturally, some said they was *painters*, too, but I doubt it. Also, just because the levee was there didn't mean the river was anywhere near it. Sometimes the river itsef was miles from the levee, and sometimes it was not far from it at all. Although that didn't keep the whole fukkin place from bein' under water every year or so, and all the animals would come up on top of the levee. One year, everybody was put'n food out on top of the levee for the wild turkeys because everything on the other side was flooded. I mean, that water was right on *up* there. But that was mostly in the spring, and at the time of the thing I'm tellin' about, it was the middle of winter and was dry as a church.

Plus, a lot of the woods out there hadn't never been cut. It was a helluva place, bar' pits, blow holes, and quicksand. Hunters got lost over 'cross the levee with some frequency, and if you didn't watch your step you could just flat-ass disappear.

That near 'bout happened to Voyd and me. It was one nem cold clear days, and we was walkin' alongside a bar' pit not far from the bottom of the levee, over in the woods. All of a sudden, I seen him. He was walkin' real slow in the same direction we was walkin, over on the other side of the bar' pit. I had a rifle, and I shoulda just popped him then and there, but I didn't. Hell, we coulda th'own him back off in there somewhere, and he wouldna never been found. But somehow, it just seemed too fukkin easy, and I wuddn get'n the rush out of the situation I had expected. I guess I didn't want it to be over.

Anyhow, Voyd seen him, too, and he lit out so as to go around the bar' pit and cut him off, but I decided I'd go across the gotdamn thing, and that was my big mistake. It looked dry, and the bottom of it was covered over with dead leaves, so I didn't have no reason to suspect it wuddn all right. But, I had no more'n got out twenty yards in the middle of that thing than I sunk down to my fukkin thighs, and I couldn't get loose. Plus, I was sinkin' deeper, and that scared the shit out of me. It's one thing to get stuck in the mud, but when you can't get out and it's more or less actively swallowing your ass, it's fukkin scary. I mean, everything was fine until, blam, all of a sudden, I couldn't get loose.

I had lost sight of Shaw, and I didn't see Voyd nowhere. Both of 'em had disappeared, and I was about to do the same, so I hollered, "Voyd! Voyd! Where the fuk are you?" No Voyd. I'm up to my nuts by now, and no gotdamn Voyd.

Then I see him, Shaw, I mean. Straight ahead of me, right where I was goin' in the first place, there he is, squat'n up on the bank of the bar' pit in that big-ass bathrobe just lookin' at me, not doin' nothin, just lookin'. I found out later Voyd was hide'n and watchin' the whole thing, the little piss-ant.

Then I really got scared, too, because Shaw stands up and picks up a fukkin tree limb. Oh, shit, I thought. That sumbich is goin' to knock my brains out with that thing. And he stepped right out onto the bottom of the bar' pit and was comin' at me. Stuck as I was, and sinkin' deeper, I just looked at him and kept

on callin' for Voyd. The funny part of it is that I had my rifle. I
had kept a'hold of it and had been mostly concerned with
keepin' it out of the mud. But I didn't do nothin' except holler
for that numbnut Voyd and look straight at that insane
muthafukka comin' 'cross the floor of the bar' pit toward me
carryin' that tree limb. Hell, me holdin' a deer rifle at port arms
and stuck up to my snubnose in quicksand, I musta looked a lot
crazier than that wild-eyed-lookin' sumbich. Besides, and I
couldn't figure this one out, he wuddn sinkin' in no mud when
he come walkin' out there towards me—and he had to come
more'n half way across the thing to get to where I was.

Anyway, he musta hit me in the fukkin head because the
next thing I know Voyd is pullin' me up the bank by one hand,
and, in the other hand, I'm holdin' on to that tree limb. And
when I looked back out to where I had been stuck in the
quicksand, I seen my deer rifle layin' out on top of the leaves in
the middle of the bar' pit. But I wuddn about to go back out
there and get it—it belonged to the county anyhow. So I just
said fukkit and decided I was just gonna say that crazy sumbich
Shaw had took it and was now armed and dangerous. I knew it
wouldn't be long before the bar' pit would be full of water, so I
wuddn too worried anybody else would see it.

Well, there was no sign of Shaw. He had run off in the
woods somewhere, and that's the last I ever saw of him, I think.
However, that was the incident that convinced me and Voyd
that he was hide'n out on the other side of the levee, so, for some
time after that, we spent a lot of the taxpayers' money runnin
around in them woods between the levee and the river checkin'
out reports that the "crazy man" had been seen scarin' the shit
out of hunters and teenagers and other people who needed for
one reason or another to be out there either on top of, or down
across, the levee. You see, except for hunters, most people who

wanted to be alone, so to speak, with one another would generally go out over the levee to park. They'd do it during the day or at night, it didn't matter. Although at night they usually stayed up on the road on top of the levee, or they went out to Mhoon's Landing and fukked in the car. But they didn't much go down into the woods at night.

See, we didn't have no motels in nem days. Meffis or Clarksdale was the closest you could get to anything like that, and, even then, somebody you knew was bound to see you and bring back the news to the coffee drinkers at the Boll and Bloom Cafe.

But, to finish out what I was telling about, on the way back to the patrol car at the foot of the levee, we come up on two nigga rabbit hunters. They knew who we was, and one of 'em looked at me kinda funny, like he wanted to laugh but wuddn goin to. We said, "Hi-yawl." And they said, "Hi-yawl, Mis' Junior, Mistuh Voyd," and that was that. The only thing I thought was a little out of place was that niggas didn't generally hunt rabbits over on the wet side of the levee. They mostly stuck to the fields on the dry side. Plus they usually had dogs, and these two boys didn't.

I figured a lot of things out years later, mainly because I never stopped turning it all over and over in my head. Of course, all the time, don't you see, Shaw was snuggled up in that silo miles and miles away from the levee, back out east of town, but we kept get'n reports of sightings out in the opposite direction, and we had to investigate 'em. It took me and Voyd quite a while to turn our attention back out towards Casequarter's Store and the Beat Line Road again. But Bone Face and his niggas was the ones that kept us away from that part of the county. It was them that phoned in most of the so-called sightings that had Voyd and me ride'n out toward the river all the fukkin time; only we didn't realize it then. Shaw was obviously out there once and maybe one or two times more than that, but mostly I think he stayed pretty near the silo. At least that's what I have come to believe about it.

One of the things that does still bother me is that business about the footprints Bone Face told Miss Helena about—how Leland Shaw's tracks just disappeared for no good reason, into thin fukkin air. I'll say one thing: it was mighty gotdamn strange the way he walked out across that bar' pit over all that quick- sand—or maybe there was just one little ol' spot where the quicksand was, and I hit it. But I fukkin doubt it. To this day I feel like there was something strange about it. 'Course, he was completely insane, and crazy people can do some pretty strange stuff, or so they say. Well, hell, that's why they call 'em crazy. But I guess they do stuff they can't actually do mostly because they don't know they can't. I don't know. Fukkum.

Shaw's tracks supposedly always disappeared around the same place. And that place was right in there where the old trail from Beaver Dam goes out east and takes up again the other side of the Coldwater River at a place called Low Gap. You can still see the imprint of that old trail here and there off to the side of the road, in the woods, and out across't a field, if you knew what to look for. But you can see it real good from the air. I got Jack Smiley to fly me around in his crop duster, and I seen it plain as fukkin day—though you wouldna necessarily knowed it was there if you was on the ground. The county engineer said it was the main route into here, as he put it, "since time began" and that a good bit of the road between Austin and and the hills was laid over it. Lawyer Montgomery said he believed the old trail was the route took by DeSoto when he come down here and discovered the Mississippi River. Could be. Hell, every city and fukkin hole in the road between Meffis and Vicksburg claims to be the place where that spic-ass Mexican muthafukka discovered the Mississippi. If you want my opinion, it was more likely the Mississippi River discovered *him*—that sumbich'll reach out and get your ass. Anyway, if what that nigga who used to work for Bone Face told me was true, it was right at the old trace them tracks disappeared. The reason I believe the nigga is that he didn't know nothin' about the trail. They don't know no fukkin history. So I knew he wuddn makin' it up.

Anyhow, I'm the one that put that together, about the disappearin' footprints and the old trace. Hell, them niggas was still superstitious as them missionary-munchin' muthafukkas back in Africa is, and some of 'em was talkin' about how Shaw was the Devil and could fly. I helped that along some. A nigga'll believe anything you tell him. They scare easy, too. And I heard, later, that even Bone Face was havin' a hard time with his "rabbit hunters" because they was get'n all worked up about the story of the disappearin' footprints. But Bone Face solved the difficulty. He just made 'em all go see old Silas Wingfield, one of the four-fukkin-thousand HooDoo doctors in the county, and old Silas put a "cunjer" on 'em, spit some tobacco juice on they heads, sold 'em some Lucky Oil plus a piece of High John the Conqueror, and told them the Devil couldn't fuk with 'em no more, and they was all right after that. I'll tell you what. Them old HooDoo doctors could tell one nem black sumbiches he was gon' die before sundown, and that asshole would lie down and do it.

On the other hand, if there was a connection between them footprints disappearing and that old-timey road, I reckon I might get a few fukkin goose bumps mysef.

The thing is, couldn't none of them people who was out to save him get hold of him neither. Apparently when he was up in that silo, one, he wouldn't come out when they called him, and,

two, they was scared to go up the chute after him. So, they just
kept an eye on him as well as they could and hoped for the
fukkin best, thinkin' that, eventually, they could get him to
come on in or go with 'em or something. But, I'll tell you, goin'
up the chute was totally un-gotdamn-appealing, because he had
the jump on your ass the whole time, and you didn't know what
was wait'n for you till you got to the top, and nobody wanted to
find out. Which is why I was all for blowing the thing up. Hell,
if wuddn nobody goin' up there after him, and he wuddn
comin' out, what could I do? I used to day-dream about it the
way some little fourteen-year-old might day-dream about getting his driver's license. It was that intense.

ANYWAY, FOR A TIME THERE, Bone Face's "helpers" kept me
and Voyd pretty busy. They musta spent every wakin' moment
cookin' up shit for us to do. Like the time when we had
organized a whole buncha good ol' boys and was gonna go out
across the fields lookin' for some sign of Shaw—and we was
goin' not real far from where the silo was, too. Well, just before
we loaded up to go out there, a call comes in from one of Bone
Face's juke joints out on the road that went from the north
"Quarters" to Mhoon's Landing.
    "Mis' Junior, Mis' Junior!" That's what the caller said.
"Mis' Junior, please come out here to the Nite Al!" It was a
woman. She was talkin' about *The Nite Al Cafe & Club*. I ast her
what was the trouble, and she said, "Aw, Mis' Junior! It's Big
Johnnie Tapp outa Meffis; he say he gon' shoot up ever'body
here 'less you come out and talks to 'im—he say he won't talk to
nobody but you!" So, I had to put the posse on hold and go out
to the fukkin juke joint.
    Natcherly, Voyd went with me. I knew he wouldn't miss it
'cause he thought they might offer him some pussy, but I told

him it was fukkin unprofessional, and he said he didn't give a fuk 'cause he wuddn no professional in the first place. I said, "I heard that, muthafukka"; then off we went. And I hoped that asshole wouldn't do nothin' I was gon' regret.

It was on a Saturday, so the place was full. Some of them fukkas had been there all night and was just barely hangin' on, planning to be there till the sun come up on Sunday. The place was a lot bigger than it looked like from the road—there wuddn much around it, nothin' really. It just set all by itsef on a gravel road with a big-ass swamp across from it. Other than that, there weren't nothin' within a mile of it. And there musta been four thousand cars, all hung together with baling wire and decorated with all that shit they used to put on 'em—big old fox tails and coon tails dyed all kinds of colors, and mud flaps and lavender day-glo plastic bug shields with fukkin propellers. They loved all kinds of big long aerials, too, whippin' back and forth, but they didn't have no radios. I never could understand how they could put all that crap on their cars when half the time the gotdamn things would not run; plus, the tires never was worth a shit, neither.

Anyway, the fukkin "nightclub" rambled all over the place, and once you got inside, it was like a whole 'nother world that went on and on and *on*, and was fulla smoke and noise and grinning niggas, sayin' "Yassuh, Cap'm, please." I didn't see Bone Face nowhere, but the woman that more or less run the place for him, LuDell, come out of the crowd and said, "Mis' Junior and Mistuh Voyd! Lawd Lawd! It's good to see yawl— lemme gitchawl somethin' to eat—we got ribs, we got chicken, we got po'k shoulder—whatchawl want? Come on wid me and lemme put yawl where it's mo comfortable . . .!" She was layin' it on thick, oooeee'n and carryin' on over Voyd and me like we was just the best gotdamn thing that had happened to her all day long. She went on like that so fast we didn't have a chance to say boo turkey or go fuk a duck.

I said, "LuDell, we got a call from somebody out here who said Big Johnnie Tapp from Meffis was gonna shoot up the place unless he talked to me—and they said he said he wouldn't talk to nobody else . . ."

"Yeah," said Voyd, "that's what they said . . ."

"So we come out," I told her. And she was just standin' there lookin' at Voyd and me with this big-ass surprised look on her face. Then she busted out laughin' and said, "Big Johnnie Tapp! Law', Mis' Junior! Big Johnnie ain't no *he*. *He*'s a *she*—you know, one nem funny folks. Law', Mis' Junior! Somebody pullin' yo leg."

"Well," I said, "that's what they told us, so we come—I reckon we'll be get'n back, since they ain't no trouble."

"Nawsuh," said LuDell, "ain't no trouble. Big Johnnie Tapp, she and Bone Face, they *good* friends. Big Johnnie ain't gon' be shoot'n nobody at Bone Face' place. She do come down here, but I ain't seen her all week—she sho do look like a man, ooom oomh, I mean! Big, too. Bone Face had to make her quit tryin' to fool wit de girls—now, when she come, she bring her own girl wit her. Deez-hyeah country girls don't know nothin' 'bout that funny stuff."

We was about to leave when LuDell piped up with, "It's near 'bout supper time. How come yawl don't jes set down here in the back room and let me feed yawl sump'm real good?" I figured, well, what the fuk. I had done told the posse if we didn't show back up at the courthouse in an hour'n and a half just to go on, and I'd contact 'em later. So, by then, I knew most of 'em had gone on home or back to the Boll and Bloom to watch the fight on the TV and shoot the shit.

I looked at Voyd, and he looked back at me, and that was

that: We sat down in one of the back rooms and made up our minds to settle in and have oursefs a real good supper. At least I did. And, I swear, that's all I ever intended. But Voyd, that little fukka, he had other plans. Anyway, I guess we both forgot about chasin' after Leland Shaw for a while because, I've got to say, that pork shoulder was smellin' mighty good and woulda put any of them Meffis barbeque places to shame.

I always liked Leonard's, on Bellevue at Mclemore, myself, but it's gone now. And that's too fukkin bad, 'cause it was the best. And I ain't shit'n you. Barbeque in Meffis ain't like anywhere in the world—they was a bunch of us went to Nashville one time, and we decided to try out the number-one barbeque place up there. I asked for a jumbo-all-white-*pulled*, and the sumbich across the counter ast me where I was from. I said, "Meffis," and he said, "Then why the fuk are you buyin' barbeque in Nashville?" I got the point, and I agreed with him. The best top-of-the-line barbeque in Nashville wuddn worth a nickel compared to the bottom of the barrel in Meffis.

I'm talkin' about pork now, I ain't talkin' about none of that Western shit. They can take them gotdamn beefaloes and shove 'em up their ass. If you get out from around here, I guarantee, people don't know doodlysquat about cookin' a pig. I ain't kid'n. If Moses had come through Meffis on his way to the fukkin Promised Land, them Israelites woulda been sayin' stuff like, "Screw a buncha *manna*, muthafukka. Han' me a 'cue!"

Anyway, there me and Voyd was, at the *Nite Al Cafe & Club*, and I was get'n mighty hungry. I tried not to forget where the fuk I was, but, sometimes a man just can't think the same thing all the gotdamn time. I mean, when I was sit'n there, I forgot I hated them black muthafukkas the way I do, and I felt like I was right at home and didn't want to be nowhere else.

Then, out come Little Bit.

Little Bit was this pretty little black gal that Voyd always had something to say to. She wuddn nothin' but one of Bone Face's whores, but she was pretty, and that was the only thing that mattered—well, that and the fact that your dick might fall off if she got hold of it. Anyhow, I looked at Voyd, and I seen his tongue was hangin' out like red necktie. I could tell he was thinkin' about food, but I knew it wuddn no *bobbakew*.

Well, I shoulda said somethin', but I didn't—for two reasons: First, I couldn't get it out of my mind that the voice on the phone had sounded a helluva lot like LuDell. And, second, by then I couldna cared less 'cause I was havin' too fukkin good a time. Pretty soon I was talkin' to LuDell, eat'n up a storm, drinkin' a few bottles of Gold Crest—which was a Meffis beer, back then—and, in the middle of all of it, still tryin' to get some idea of who it was that called the Sheriff's office and got me and Voyd to come out there. To this day I would swear it was LuDell, but she denied the piss out of it and just kept sayin' shit like, "Nawsuh. Nawsuh, Mis' Junior. Now you know it weren't me. I wouldn't ne-e-ever do nothin' like that, not to you, Mis' Junior, nawsuh. You and me, we's been knowin' one another too long. Naw-*suh*. I bleeve that call had to come from some nem lil' ol' white boys up there in town—you know how they do. You 'bout have to git they daddies to take a strop to 'em."

She had a point. But, I still think the voice on that phone sounded like LuDell, and, knowin' now what I know after all these years, I say it had to be her. Anyhow, finally, I was git'n wore out with barbeque and beer, and I sho wuddn gonna stick my pecker in one nem gals—shit, I might not-a never got it back, and I'd be poppin' penicillin to this very fukkin moment I'm standin' here now. And that ain't no lie—I reckon 'bout a third of the county population had syphilis, and the other two-thirds had the clap. Back then, the government come in and give everybody a Wasserman, and then come back and give everybody a shot. And that did make a dent in it, but it didn't ever knock it out. That's one reason they was so many fukkin cockeyed people in the Delta, if you ast me. Them that didn't drink theysefs to death, fukked theysefs to death, and ever'one of 'em drove too gotdamn fast—'cept the niggas, and, like I said, their old cars wouldn't hardly run, and they mostly tried to die fukkin, which is why there was so gotdamn many of 'em.

They was a planter down around Clarksdale who heard a scream come from one of his tenant houses, and he run over there to see what was the matter and found a ninety-year-old man dead as a hammer between the legs of a nineteen-year-old gal. He was a preacher. And she was just lyin' there hollerin' till somebody come in and moved the body off her. But that's what they do. They just keep preachin' and fukkin till they fall over dead, and try not to work too hard in between. Hell, I know those coksukkas, and that's the gotdamn Gospel truth.

But where the fuk was Voyd? I got ready to go, and I realized I hadn't seen that little *scof'uh* for a long-ass time. "Where the fuk is Mister Voyd?" I ast LuDell.

"Law', Mis' Junior, where *is* he?!" she said, knowin' all along exactly where he was because she had put Little Bit up to comin' out and takin' him back off in one nem rooms somewhere. So I said, "Gotdamnit, LuDell, now show me where Mistuh Voyd is 'cause we got to git on back to town, since there ain't no trouble out here."

"I bleeve he be up in the back," she said, and I followed her off into one of the hallways where she opened a door, and there set Voyd, buck nekkid and drunk as a bicycle, playin' strip poker with Little Bit and another one named Baby Mae. They was lookin' at Voyd and laughin' their ass off while that dumb bastard was seriously tryin' to play cards.

Now what was I supposed to do? I couldn't say nothin' to him in front of them niggas. 'Course, there again, what the fuk do you say to a nekkid white man in a nigga juke joint anyway, never mind that the sumbich was a semi-law-enforcement-muthafukka and that not only was he drunk and nekkid, but his clothes was nowheres to be found—well, Little Bit handed me one of his socks and said, in one nem real sweet kinda voices, that they "didn't know *whut* Mistuh Voyd done with his things."

Well, I couldn't haul him out the way we come in. I had to go out and bring the patrol car on around behind the place. You wouldn't dare do it today, but I left the fukkin motor runnin' so it would warm up on the inside, and I come on in the back door. When I got to the room where that silly sumbich was, LuDell was knockin' the bottom out of a big cardboard box, and then she made Voyd step in it and hold it up around hissef. Bear in mind it was about two degrees outside—one nem cold, clear winter nights when there ain't no moon, and you can see ever' fukkin star in the sky, and you could *really* see 'em out there in the country away from town. Plus, I knew, too, that that crazy-ass Leland Shaw must be somewhere off in the night lookin' at 'em right then, same as I was, and that he didn't know *where* the fuk he was but that he, in his crazy-ass mind, believed he was on the road to somewhere even if it didn't exist; and me, I knew I wuddn goin' nowhere, yet I was the one that had done been sidetracked. For a minute there it didn't make no fukkin sense. But, I reckon I was just too conscientious for my own good.

Baby Mae opened the door; I looked real good, several times, up and down the fukkin hall, and when I didn't see nobody, I jerked Voyd's silly ass out of the room and pushed the sumbich through the back door. But when he tried to get into car, he kept fallin' back in the dirt because the cardboard box wouldn't cooperate, so I made the sumbich leave it layin' there and lie down in the back till I could get him to where he lived, where he staggered-ass up the front steps, nekkid. I called him a dumbsunavabitch, and he said, "Fuk you, Junior Ray. I was winnin'." And I said, "Voyd, what would it look like if somebody was to see you and me ride'n around in the middle of the fukkin' night and you nekkid?"

And he said, "They'd just think you're a queer." That really pissed me off, so I said, "You're the fukkin queer, sumbich; you're the one who's nekkid."

"Fuk you," he said and started on inside the house, but right before he closed the door, he stuck his head back out and said, "I was winnin'."

That sumbich really believed it. Voyd mighta been dumb as a stump, but he *was* sincere. And I guess that counts for something. But, now, as far as his clothes was concerned, they started showin' up on every nigga in town, and there wuddn nothin' that sumbich could say, nor me neither. They knew I couldn't tell Sheriff Holston. And they sho knew Voyd wuddn gonna let it out that he had to run out the back door of the Nite Al in a fukkin cardboard box. He was caught both ways, and so was I. One, he couldn't say that they done it to him. That would make him look like more of an asshole than he was. And, two, he couldn't say that he done it on his own, 'cause there wouldna been no answer to that, no way on this fukkin earth to explain nothin' like that. But, three, if any of it had come out, me and him woulda had to leave town.

He had to give Little Bit twenty dollars to make her stop wearin' his belt because it had his name on it. Then, old Dollar Bob, the nigga who picked up the mail at the train station every day, turned up wearin' his letter jacket. Natcherly, somebody down at the barber shop said something about it, and Voyd told 'em he give it to old Dollar Bob for some haulin' he done for him, but I don't think anybody believed it. They didn't know what was goin' on, but they didn't say nothin'.

Over the next few days, we seen his shirt and his pants and his shoes walkin' down the street, too, and them that was wearin' 'em would just look over at him and grin, and say, "Mawnin', Mistuh Voyd." And there wuddn nothin he could do about it.

"You didn't know you was gonna be the fashion king, did you, sumbich?" I said to him. But that wuddn what really bothered him. The bad part of it all was that he knew that all them niggas had seen his little old vy-eena sausage of a dick. And the truth is, I think that's what they was laughin' about the most.

It really affected him, too. He wouldn't get out of the patrol car much for a long, long time after that, and he'd just sorta sit down low and pull his baseball cap down over his eyes. Voyd was pretty sensitive about the size of his little vy-eena, but I told him it was his own gotdamn fault and served his ass right for goin' out there with pussy on his mind in the first gotdamn place— what did he think was goin' to happen if he got fukkin drunk and took his clothes off in the middle of main street, so to speak.

How'd he think that made me look? I told him he was a fukkin embarrassment to every coksukkin white man in the whole gotdamn world, especially now that half the niggas in the world—which definitely lived here in Mhoon County, Mississippi—knew what a lil' bitty weeny he had. I said, "Jezus Christ, Voyd, now them sumbiches think we're *all* like that. How the fuk am I supposed to keep those assholes in line after the stunt you done pulled?"

And that was when I stopped carryin' that little slapjack I'd been usin' and started totin' a baseball bat. After Voyd showin' his ass like he did, I just didn't feel like the slapjack was gon' get the job done no more.

I GOT UP AND WENT TO CHURCH THE NEXT DAY—I didn't usually go much back then, but I figured I needed to after what had took place the night before. I was mighty fukkin uneasy about it, and I was scared it was all gonna hit the fukkin fan. So, I went to church—they all wanted me to dedicate my life to the Lord, but I stopped short of actually sayin' I would. Hell, I just wanted to feel better about havin' been made a fukkin fool of in a nigga night club. I imagined that God woulda been pretty pissed off about me bein' in a night club, off duty, so to speak, in the first fukkin place; but I felt like he'd be double pissed if he knowed it was fulla niggas.

Anyhow, the preacher wuddn too bad. The sign on the outside of the church said LET JESUS BE YOUR RABBIT'S FOOT. I ain't never forgot it. And, to this very fukkin day, I do let Jesus be my lucky piece. Well, I do and I don't. When you come down to it, I feel a lot luckier with a .38 in my pocket than I do with Jesus, wherever the fuk he is.

Moreover, I cannot say that all I wanted was to kiss;
cannot say that all I wanted, at that time, was to touch;
nor can I say that what I wanted
was to believe she loved me,
as I, indeed, believed I loved her,
though there is no question,
as it turns out,
that there can be a great deal of difference between belief
and truth;
yet, given a choice,
either will do
at two in the morning.

No, what I wanted at that protracted moment was to

become lost in the cellular structure of her flesh, to disperse, too, and blend suspended with the smell of her skin and to swim, one-eye-closed, through the heavy, long, hot silk of her hair like thick winter grass. I wanted death and life as one, which, at certain peaks must be the aim of love and that, too, even when it is not love at all; because touch is beyond love, and it is the only thing that can free love or lust from the sterility of an abstract. Without touch, love is a dream without a dreamer and the name of pleasure that cannot be enjoyed.

Oh, passion is not the word.
What I sought was greater than that.
Passion, I say, is ordinary compared
to the nameless transcendence I was after.
I wanted time and no time alike
to hold me there forever,
without food or clothing or even breath;
I wanted the snuffing out and the snuffing in
of some cosmic, brahmanic sensuality,
and I wanted the desire I had become
to consume the universe –

yet, kissing was all it was, and now I know that had there been more, with Kimbrough, it would not have been enough, because, though at the time I may not have been able to articulate it in quite this way, it was never what I wanted; and I did not know that.

5

MR. FLOPPY — THE NEED TO SHOOT SOMEBODY — LOST IN THE WOODS ACROSS THE LEVEE — A SUBMARINE — BOY SPROUTS — MR. BRAINSONG

Holy Mackrel!
Hooty Dooty Dooty
Smoke me a fish
And catch me some booty!

I MENTIONED THAT WOMAN I SEE OVER NEAR SLEDGE. Lately I wonder if I can keep that up. I do like her and ever'thing, but, to tell you the fukkin truth, she's got ways about her that mightnear drive me out of my mind—and I don't mean with *luv*, neither.

Lately she's done taken to givin' names to body parts—you know, like she calls a finger a pinky, a toe a piggy, and a butt a popo or some such shit as that. And it goes on: feets is dogs, tits are buhppies, teeth are toofies, stomachs is tumtums—mostly the same old shit you've heard all your life from one silly-ass sunavabitch or another, usually some tweety-tweet fukkin woman.

It's enough to gag a gotdamn maggot. The fukkin latest is we had done eat us one of the best gotdamn suppers you ever saw—I mean, I put down a washtub full of bream and hushpuppies, and a case of beer—and we was in the bed, and I was conked out—it was late on a Saturday night, about two in the mornin' I'd guess—and I feel her tappin on my back. I thought, what the fuk? What in the hell does that woman want this time of night? I ain't twenty-seven no more, so I do like to get some sleep, especially when I've eat so much that late in the evenin'. I mean, even your larger animals have to sleep off a big meal, like one nem snakes you see on TV after they swallow a goat. That sumbich lays there like a gotdamn nylon with a ham in it and don't even *begin* to move for a long fukkin time until he needs go swallow another goat. Well, that's the way I was.

Pretty soon there it come again. *Tap tap tappytap.* And naturally I said, "What the gotdamn fuk do you want?" Only I added "Honey" on to it. And she says, "Miz Squint wants to go dancin with Mr. Floppy."

Well, fuk, that scared the shit outa me. I thought they was somebody else in the house I didn't know about. So I said, "Miz Squint and Mr. Floppy? Who the fuk are they?"

Then she puts on this coksukkin little girl's voice, which makes me want to fukkin th'ow-up, and says, "Miz Squint wants Mr. Floppy to wake up and shake *ha-yends*"—God I hate that shit, especially when an old bat tries to sound like a fukkin majorette—bear in mind all this bullshit is goin' on at two in the gotdamn morning—and then I feel her reachin' over and grabbin' a-hold of my dick. And it ain't in no better shape than I am. Well, normally, that'd been all right, but *gotdamn!* I was so fukkin knocked out from eat'n all them bream that shakin' hands with Mr. Floppy was about last on my list. But, hell, as long as it was her that was doin' all the shakin, it was all right with me and Mr. Floppy for the time bein'.

Well, that didn't last long. I don't know about Mr. Floppy, but I had done dozed back off when she come on with, "Oooh, that was nice. Does Mr. Floppy want to shake hands with Miz *Squee-yennt*?"—and, see, I still didn't catch on to who the fuk Miz Squint was. Then, before me or Mr. Floppy could say hell no or go fuk yoursef, she flies straight up in the gotdamn air, lands on her knees, and with this wild-ass look on her face, hauls my butt over on my back, throws one nem thighs across't me, straddles my ass, and commences to brush that big old industrial-size pussy of hers back and forth over the top of Mr. Floppy. And I'm pinned to the fukkin Posturepedic.

"Miz Squint just loooooves Mr. Floppy-woppy," she said. I hate to admit it but Mr. Floppy-fukkin-woppy was totally unimpressed. And so was I. But, by now, I knew who Miz Squint was. And I was about to tell her to go fuk the elektrolux, or that gotdamn poodle, who'd done jumped up there with her and had his cold-ass nose stuck up between her butt and Mr. Floppy's balls.

Pretty soon, though, Mr. Floppy, I guess because he was a little closer to the situation than I was, started kinda get'n in step with Miz Squint. You might say he began to cut a fukkin rug. That's a joke. Anyway, it was mill-whistle time in the loggin' camp for Mr. Floppy, and Miz Squint has done gone from zero to sixty in about a minute and a half. And I look up, and the woman has her neck and her face stretched way up towards the ceiling and her arms straight down on my shoulders while the rest of her from the waist down is movin faster than a fukkin blue blur and flippin' Mr. Floppy all *over* the gotdamn place. I mean her and Miz Squint together coulda made a fortune shinin' shoes at the shoe factory. But, Mr. Floppy, by now, he's right in the middle of it, if you know what I mean, and Miz Squint is eat'n it up. That's another joke.

That big old fat ass is slappin' and blappin' up and down on my thighs like a flat tire on blacktop road. I mean this whole

thing had done took on a kinda unreal look, and it was like I was
just set'n back an watchin' it without actually havin' nothin' to
do with it. Hell, that wuddn anything new 'cause Mr. Floppy
always did have a mind of his own anyhow. However, he didn't
always use it, and I think you could say the same about Mr.
Floppies all over the fukkin world, that they are prone to trouble
and easily led. Well, fuk, a hard dick has no conscience. And the
Sledge woman, man, she wuddn fukkin—she was flyin'. I mean
fukkin *airborne*. All she needed was a pair of goggles.

Then, all of a sudden, she and Miz Squint come to a
screechin' dead-ass stop in mid-air, and she sat there, stiff as a
two-by-four, and stayed thatta way for about ten seconds without sayin' a word or let'n out a sound of any sort, and then she
just collapsed and come *kablump* down on top of me and laid
there like a truck-load of tapioca or something until she kinda
tilted and I kinda shoved her over to the left toward her side of
the bed. And that's the last I heard anything *that night* about Miz
Squint or Mr. Floppy.

Later on, another time, she wanted to get a book and read
the marriage ceremony so Miz Squint and Mr. Floppy could
"have a Tom Thumb wedding." I started to go along with it
because I figured that would be the best way I knew of to not
have to go through all that shit no more, because, if Miz Squint
and Mr. Floppy was to get married, that woulda been the last
Miz Squint-and-Mr. Floppy sockhop I'd have to sit through at
two in the gotdamn morning, for sure. Any sumbich knows
marriage is the fukkin death of romance—well, romance is
actually the death of itsef, if you ask me.

You know how that is. People start off hotter than a pepper
sprout and in six months find out they not only don't like one
another, they don't even *know* each other; yet, there they are
signed up, sealed, and de-fukkin-livered. Thinkin' back, I re-

member I was in love a whole lots of fukkin times, but, of course, when you come right down to it, not with anybody I ever knew. And that includes Des.

I ain't no expert, but I do know that when you are hangin' around some woman and sex gets to be a fukkin chore, that just means one gotdamn thing, and that is you're not pluggin the one you ought to be hooked up to and visa-fukkin-versa.

But, I reckon, until something better comes along, I'm not gon' change horses in the middle of the Coldwater River. She's all right, and, when I'm in the mood, I like a good bounce as much as any sumbich. On the other hand, maybe Des was right that night down at the MoonLite Drive-In. Maybe, if the truth was known, and I'm not sayin this is it, maybe I *would* druther fart than fuk. But that don't make me out of line with the rest of the world because when you look in the papers and on the TV, whenever there's anything truly important goin on, like a war, it ain't never over a piece of pussy. Oh, they may claim it is, like in that famous war they named the rubbers after, but it ain't, and that's a fukkin fact. Although it does have something to do with what country's got the biggest dick and can out-piss the others.

But I guess it don't do no good to be right if you ain't rich. And, if you're rich, you don't need to be right. So fukkit.

AND, ANOTHER THING: God's a white man. Hell, that's one reason I started goin' to church. I mean, look here, Jesus was a white man—judgin' by ever pitcher I ever saw of him; plus, he was a Jew, and most of them is white, and he was the son of God. Right? Right. 'Cause the fukkin Bible don't lie. Plus, Mary was a Jew, too, so she had to be a white girl, and, as we know, she was the mama of Jesus. There-fukkin-fore, it don't take a coksukkin genius to work that out. If a boy is white—I mean really white—then his mama and daddy has to be white. So that's why I say

God is a white man. And if he ain't, he sure as hell acts like one.

AND SOMETHING ELSE, I was watchin' TV the other evenin'
over at Sledge, and they was one nem psychiatrists goin on about
how they's thousands and thousands of people out there that
suffers from feelings of guilt. Well, that just knocked me back.
He went on to name off a whole slough of shit all these
thousands of muthafukkers done and are feelin' guilty about—
causing them, he said, to have all sorts of mental as well as
physical problems. And I thought, holy shit, I'd give my left nut
to do all them things, and there them assholes are, payin' a
coksukka like that psy-fukkin-chiatrist all their hard and otherwise earned money 'cause they feel bad about get'n to do 'em. It
didn't make no fukkin sense. And I'm set'n there get'n more and
more pissed by the fukkin second 'cause I never got to do *none*
of them things on the list a muthafukka's supposed to feel guilty
about. Hell, I never felt guilty about a gotdamn thing in my
whole life and don't expect to.

There's something wrong with a coksukka that feels bad
about doin' stuff that ought to be fun, long as he can get away
with it. I tell you, I don't lose sleep over nothing this world has
to offer, as long as it don't cause me no inconvenience. I get
plumb sick of hearin' these sumbiches on the television talk
about love and guilt and bein' sensitive. Horseshit. I know what
makes the world go 'round. Fukkin bullets. That's what. And I
ain't had nothin' to drink neither.

Now, I believe I have wanted to kill things ever since I can
remember. It didn't matter what it was, turtles on a log, snakes,
bugs, stray dogs; I got a thrill out of poppin' it with a .22. But all
along, as I growed up, I knew that what I really wanted to do was
to shoot a man—and get away with it. Well, the Delta is a fairly
violent-ass place. White men used to kill niggas down here and

never say boo-turkey to nobody. Hell, on them old levee gangs, if trouble come up and the cap'n had to blast a couple of them black bastards, they just tho-d 'em in the dirt and made 'em part of the pile and kept on workin'. And wuddn nobody nowhere gon' say nothin' to them white men about it. I hate it I wuddn born back in them times—although the times I come up in wuddn a whole lot different, I'll say that.

It wuddn much different when white men killed each other or when niggas killed each other. Most of the time there wuddn no trial and nothin' ever happened to nobody. They just kept on plantin' cotton, 'cause that was the only thing that really mattered. With white men, one killin' another was considered just a personal thing, so the law preferred to stay out of it. And when a nigga killed another nigga, it depended on who each of 'em was and who was the most valuable to what planter. But even if none of that applied, the law still didn't get worked up over two niggas killin' one another on Saturday night just as long as both of those muthafukkas was back in the field Monday morning. That's a joke.

But I guess you had to be there.

Well, hell, look at the state penitentiary. Those sumbiches used to get Christmas furloughs! Plus, the guards with the guns weren't *guards*, they was *trusties*, but, if you was just a regular convict and tried to run off, they'd blow your ass off in a minute. And a lot of them *trustie* gunmen lived in houses on the side of Highway 49 with their families. Shoot, Mississippi was the first state to allow married couples to get together—on Sunday, too! And them fukkin convicts even had 'em a system back then called "brother-in-lawin'" whereby if I was in prison and my wife come to see me on the weekend, she could bring a girl friend and say it was her sister, and you could be my "brother in law" and get to shack up same as I would.

All that sounds fine, but them sumbiches had to work harder than a water boy in hell, and I wouldna wanted no part of it because of that. Otherwise, it didn't sound too bad.

Mississippi used to be able to do whatever it wanted to do, until the United States found out about it. And now that Mississippi has become part of the United States, things ain't the same. Well, it's become *partially* part of it, anyway. Which is sayin' a lot, because, when I was a boy, wuddn none of it in America.

So maybe, in a funny way, I can kinda see why that crazy-ass Leland Shaw didn't believe he was home. Ever'thing was changin'. Just like old people dyin', time takes away the signposts, so, after the war, things didn't look the same, didn't sound the same . . . didn't want no more to be the same—and the place itsef didn't even really know or even barely understand that it didn't mind changin' . . . or that it wuddn get'n a hell of a lot out of the old way nohow. So fukkit. It was gonna change and did. Well, in his shot-up brain, he just saw it clearer than the rest of us.

And the bigshots? There ain't no pleasure in having power when it really ain't yours no more. It was get'n to be the government's. So, in a sense, them planters became the businessmen they always was anyhow and got rid of the niggas and replaced 'em with radios and computers and the biggest fukkin' machines you ever laid you eyes on, so that with no more'n four drivers they could farm thousands of acres and never step down in the dirt. These huge-ass farms just became factories without no walls. The Americans had done zeroed in on our ass and slapped us with a new day.

None of this horseshit happened overnight. In fact, it's just mostly in lookin' back that I can see it at all. The thing is, I have noticed that a lot of momentous events tend to slip by unnoticed, and I believe this here social change crap is kinda like when you're lyin' up there on the Posturepedic smokin' a cigarette after dippin' your pole in the slough. There ain't no immediate sign that anything has changed. It's quite a bit of time later that you discover your little frog giggin' expedition has produced you a fukkin tadpole, and *that's* when you realize that a while back you participated in a momentous event and didn't even know it.

And so it was with me and Leland Shaw. I still aim to shoot somebody, sometime, somewhere, somehow, before I die; but I guess it ain't gonna be *that* crazy muthafukka.

Chr*EYE*st, it's been over thirty-five years since all that stuff happened. Almost ever'body around here that had anything to do with it is dead, and if that asshole Leland Shaw *is* alive, then he's got to be over seventy. Me, I'm sixty-two. So, there's just been too much time and too much gone, and I know I ain't never gonna find him now. Hell, I ain't even gonna look for him. I reckon, in a way, the pure-dee desire to kill the sumbich is almost as good as the thing itself—since memories is about all anybody ever winds up with anyhow; and, even though memories is in the past, they *did* happen, and for that reason alone, they's a whole lot more to 'em than, say, the water in the wake of your average bass boat. But, oh hell ol' Bill, if I could just have one more chance to do one or two things different! I'd give my right nut—no, I wouldn't neither; I'd give some other sumbich's right nut. But, *I'd* do ever' bit of the work of catchin' him and holdin' him down to get it.

Peed I'ma lunkin
Peed I'ma lye
Peed I'ma lunkin
Punkin pie!

Issa hissa hucka
Duvva kucka wye
Peed I'ma lunkin
Punkin pie!

We sat there just inside, on the edge of a darkening wood of broadleaf and cypress in the late December afternoon during deer season, he, my father, in the branches of a maple and I, beside him, in the fork of an elm. But he had become lost and far away in the sounds and small events of the forest. He did not carry a gun. I was the hunter then, and it was I who would be smeared with the blood of the buck after the kill, by my uncles and my cousins – or I whose shirt-tail would be sheared, for shooting at and missing the kill. But on that day neither took place. My father and I sat and watched, and I did not shoot, nor did he indicate to me that he wanted me to, even when, at one time, five doe and a spike trotted beneath us, as though he may have felt that silence and beauty, far better than blood or humiliation, would mark me more irrefutably as a man.

ANYWAY, FOR THE LONGEST TIME, we still thought he was out over 'cross the levee—later, of course, we knew he wuddn and zeroed in on the area around the silo, but, well, fuk, things take time.

We got two reports of somebody seein' the "maniac" out at Hawk Lake—which was over on the wet side of the levee on a big piece of land that had the Cut-off on one side of it and the Mississippi River on the other. Why the fuk he'd a'been out there I do not know, but that was the word, so we had to go check it out. By "we" I mean Voyd and me.

Hawk Lake was sump'm. It was surrounded by them big-ass cypresses the niggas call lawdgods, 'cause they say only the

"Lawd God" knows how old they are. They were big. And them fukkin woods out there was *vast*. It was all part of a hunt'n club and still is today, but, back then, the members was local people, and today it's Meffis people. The owners was from up in Meffis, and one day they come down and kicked out all the local people and sold memberships to all their Meffis buddies for thousands of fukkin dollars, *And,* I heard, cut down most of the fukkin trees and built a gotdamn big-ass clubhouse. But, back then, it was different. Once't you got back in nem woods, muthafukka, you was lost in time. And you didn"t need no fukkin clubhouse.

So we go out there. We went to Evansville, hung a right, and cut a trail on the blacktop to Austin where we got up on the levee and rode south, past Grindle Lake, till we got to the place you turn off onto to go down on the other side of the levee into the Hawk Lake woods. It was about ten-thirty in the morning.

All we had heard was that the "maniac" had been sighted beyond the lake, out toward Spike's Bayou and Stump Island. That meant we had to drive in as far as we could and then get out and start walkin'. The patrol car made it pretty good till just past the lake, and then it was too rough for it, so that was that, and we left it there, right in the middle of the little old log road, right by where a buncha wild hogs had been root'n up the ground off to the side of it.

They was a whole lot of them suckas over there, but they was quick to get wind of you, and when they did, they was gone. It was almost impossible to sneak up on 'em, unless you come up from down wind, but they'd hear you 'fore they saw you or smelled you. That's why most people hunted 'em with dogs. In fact, one sumbich used a couple of Catahoula Curs, and I heard that was the best kinda dog to have if you was goin' after wild pigs. I seen one of two of them boars brung out of there over five hunnerd pounds and tuskses long as your fukkin forearm. The sumbiches get so lean and tough and ugly once they go wild they looks more like a coksukkin wolf than they do a pig. And they was all brown and white and white and black, 'cause they was just regular old Durocs and Poland Chinas and barnyard hogs that had got loose and took to livin' in the woods. But, after a generation, son, they was some wild muthafukkas.

Finally, of course, by the end of the fifties, they was bein' hunted to death, and then, after 1965, they weren't none. There never was a real season on 'em, so there wuddn no control over hunt'n 'em the way there oughta have been.

I reckon by then it was get'n to be about 11:15.

"How the fuk are we supposed to find a gotdamn thing out here, Junior Ray?" asked Voyd. And he had a point. I truly didn't know what to do, so I said, "Let's just be real still for a few minutes, Voyd, to see if we hear anything."

"Aw-ight," he said. "Aw-ight."

Well, that didn't produce no results, so we started to walk off into the brush, figuring we'd come out on the river; then, we'd turn around and come back. But that's not how it worked out, and I don't know where the fuk we went wrong, I guess, by then, we thought we was expert maniac hunters, after the hoppin' man and after that run-in with Shaw in the bar' pit.

We walked for a mighty long way, dodgin' limbs and payin' more attention to the ground than we was to where we was goin'. But we wuddn ready to say we was lost. Them woods was deep, and it was get'n late in the day. Then we heard somethin'. It was a kind of rustlin' ahead of us—whatever it was would rustle a little and then stop and then rustle some more. We didn't want to keep walkin' and just walk up on it, not knowin' what the fuk it was, so Voyd picked up a piece of wood and chunked it real hard into a buncha cane straight in front of us. And it went "kabong."

"Shit," we said, both at the same time. And Voyd th'owed another stick of wood, harder than the first one, into the cane, and "kabong," there it come again. "Kabong." I mean, a person would expect to hear just about anything back in them woods except "ka-fukkin-*bong*." Obviously whatever it was was metal. But we knowed it couldn't be no jeep or nothin' because there wuddn no road nor no way one coulda got back there. Plus, we sho as hell knew it weren't no waterheater. But there was no denyin' that Voyd had been th'owin' at something made out of iron or tin or steel—unless they was some kinda fukkin tree called a kabong-nut. That's a *joke*.

Anyhow, there wuddn nothin' to do but find out what it was, so, with a good deal of caution, we went up to the cane and looked in it—it really wuddn all that thick—and there, big as a freight train was a gotdamn gigantic rusty-ass thing longer than a mule dick which, at first, we didn't know what it was—hell, it was huge—and, then, we seen it was a fukkin submarine, set'n up there in them woods dry as a bone.

Well, it looked like we was in part of the old river bed; but, remember, it was, as I have said, the middle of a cold-ass winter, and high water wuddn gon' be anything to worry about that year until probably the last of March or the first of April. But there sho had been some high fukkin water one time or another to put that thing up in them woods like that. And that wuddn all. It was a coksukkin *German* submarine—well, I say it was, I mean, I didn't see one nem whatchamacallit swastikas on it nowhere, but I did see some words on some dials and stuff when I shined my light down inside it, and they was a lot of G's and Z's. It was definitely not no American words on them things. Anyhow, when I seen it, it just about took my breath away, and I guess it did Voyd's too.

There was a big sycamore that had fell over on it, so we

climbed up on the tree trunk and got up on top of the thing, but we did not go down inside it. We did try to look through one or two of them hatches that was open on the deck; but, even though we had our flashlights, we still couldn't see much— except them dials I mentioned. Mostly, though, we just wondered where the muthafukkas who was on it went to. Bear in mind, the war had done been over for fourteen years. I was just fukkin stunned, but all Voyd could think about was souvenirs.

Naturally, I got real interested in the guns. They was a big one on the deck in front of the tall part, and they was what looked to be about a .50-caliber machine gun up in the tall part. The whole thing was rusted all to hell, but even the cables was still up—one goin' from the tall part to the front, where there was a kinda jaggedy-ass looking doojigger stickin' up, and there was two cables runnin' from the tall part to the rear end, and there weren't no gun on the back part. Well, hell, it looked like all of 'em you ever seen in the movies, only it was really something to actually be up on one. I don't know if it was or was not a German submarine, but I do know one gotdamn thing: that was a helluva place to leave a boat.

Another thing I do know, and that is there was a German prisoner of war camp at Como, just up in the Hills, and there was another one a little ways down the road near Rosedale, which sets there right at the bottom of the levee. Now, it may be those sukkas thought they was at Rosedale, and they meant to get in there and bust one of their buddies out or something; fuk if I know. But, nevertheless, there it was. And it wouldn't surprise me if the muthafukkas hadn't married majorettes and was farmin' cotton right this fukkin' minute. That's what I'da done.

Now, while I was lookin' all around up on top of the thing, Voyd had done got back down on the ground, and I had done lost sight of him until I hear: "Hey, Junior Ray! Looka here at this!" Well, I rubberneck over the side, and there that little fukka is, holdin' up a lillo-bitty pig—and it's squealin' like a sumbich. "Looka here, Junior Ray! Ain't he cute?" he said. And just about the time he said "cute," the biggest, ugliest, maddest sow you ever saw come bellowin' out of the cane. Voyd took one look at them teeth, and screamed "Holy Shit!" and th'owed that little pig straight at her.

Then, I swear to you, he leapt up on top of that submarine where I was like he was a gotdamn kanga-fukkin-roo—I mean, I ain't never seen nothin' like it on TV . . . well, it wuddn exactly like that, because he done a good bit of clawin' and scramblin' too, and I had to reach over and grab his hand and give him a pull, but what you got to remember is that there weren't nothin' on the side of that thing to grab a'hold of, and, if it hadna been for that big sycamore leanin' over on it, we couldna got up there in the first place. *But,* when the sow come out of the cane, Voyd wuddn on the side where the tree was. And that's why it was so amazing.

On the other hand, fear is a helluva fuel. And if a man's got enough of it, he can always get where he's goin'. Anyway, we wuddn movin' nowhere for a while, not till we could be sure that old sow wuddn nowhere around. But, of course, now we knew what had been doin' the rustlin' we had heard in the first place.

Quite some time after it had got dark, we come down and started walkin' in the direction we thought would take us back to the log road. It didn't, and we knew we was lost bigger'n shit.

Well, we walked until we was about to fukkin drop, stumblin' over sticks and dodgin' limbs—seemed like our lights made everything darker than it woulda been anyhow. After the longest time, we come to a halt and set down at the bottom of a big old tree, and it was there, when we had been there just a few seconds, that we heard some voices and seen a light flickerin' off through the underbrush.

It turned out to be a buncha Boy Sprouts, and they was by theysefs and didn't have the sproutmaster, Tommy Bland, with 'em—he brought 'em out in his pickup, and he was gonna return the next day and take 'em back in to town. Ain't no sense tryin' to describe what their little camp was like, 'cause there ain't a sumbich alive that don't know—and if he don't, then where's the muthafukka been all his gotdamn life, some fukkin liberry?

Anyhow, Voyd and me made out like we was just out there in the woods checkin' on 'em to make sure they was all right, when, the fact is, we didn't know where in the shit we was. But we was sly about it, and we ast 'em whichaway they come in, and they said they come in the log road and pointed off in the woods, and one of 'em said, "Yeah, and we seen yawl's car out there before we got to where we're at."

Me and Voyd told 'em we was out there on other business, too, and had had to check out some things which was better done on foot, and that's why we left the car—which, of course, we had no fukkin idea where it was and was hopin' the little dicklickers would tell us without us havin' to ask.

Then, one little scownbooger ast us, "Are yawl lookin' for the maniac?"

I said, "Well, that *is* one reason we're out here. They was a report that somebody thought they seen him this mornin' in this vicinity—yawl ain't come across nothin', have you?"

"Naw*suh,* Mister Loveblood, we ain't seen nothin', but we mighta *heard* him," one of 'em piped up.

And another said, "Yassuh, we been hearin' stuff all night, but we all got our machetes," and he and all the rest of 'em helt up the gotdamndest collection of fukkin blades you ever laid your eyes on this side of a nigga crap game.

"Well," said Voyd, "yawl sho look like you come prepared, but I don't reckon you're gonna need them big *swo*-rds tonight, 'cause I think, if the maniac *was* here, he's done moved on; only, just to ease your mind, Mister Loveblood and me, we don't think he was never here in the first place—but be careful and don't run up on none nem wild hogs, specially them mama pigs, you hear?"

And they all said, "Yassuh, Mister Mudd," 'cause that was Voyd's name, Voyd Mudd, like *mud* only with two d's. I noticed a couple of them little fukkas looked at each other kinda funny, but they didn't say nothin. They was planters' boys, and I figured they'd heard they daddies say somethin' once't in a while about Voyd and me—like, oh, them two assholes don't know what the fuk they're doin' or some such shit as that, so naturally them kids of theirs wouldn't have no respect for us. But I didn't really give a shit about that. I just wanted to get the fuk outa them woods and go home.

I still didn't know how we was gonna get back to the patrol car, but old Voyd solved the problem. He looked real serious at them little Boy Sprouts and said, "Aw-ight, now, just to make sure yawl can han'l yoursefs, I'mo test yawl. I bet nair'a one of you can find the log road in the dark—and if you can, I still betcha none of you can tell whichaway the patrol car is."

Well, hell, I mean the hands went up. They was all for showin' us what smart ass Boy Sprouts they was and commenced to yappin', "Yas*suh!* Yas*suh!* It's thissa way. Follow us!" And we did, and that's how we located the fukkin' car. I do believe we fooled most of 'em, but, even if we didn't fool 'em all, they was too well brought up to say anything about it. However, I noticed them two planters' boys look at one another in that "what-the-fuk-is-goin'-on" way one mo' time.

YET, I DON'T KNOW. Miss Florence and some of the others at
the courthouse the next day seemed to think something was
mighty fukkin funny, and they was all smilin' when I got to
work, and I had that kinda creepy-ass feelin' you get when you
think somebody has somethin' on you.

"Did you find the maniac, Junior Ray?" Miss Florence ast
me.

"No, ma'm," I said. "But we found something else near
'bout as good."

"Uh-huhn," she said. "And what was that?" And she looked
like she was gonna pee in her fukkin shoe.

"We found a submarine," I said. "And I think it was a
German one." That kinda stopped her for a second or two dead
in her tracks, like somebody done unplugged her ass in the back
of her head.

"You and Voyd found a what?" she said. "A *what?*"

"A submarine," I told her—only I really wanted to say, "A
gotdamn fukkin submarine, you shit-eat'n bitch!" But, naturally, I couldn't say nothin' like that to the old Baptist buttsniffer.
She always thought she was better'n me and smarter'n ever'body
else. Well, fukher. What if she was. I didn't give a shit. She was
the kinda woman they always make principal, the kind you can't
never get over on because they know you know they never will
think you're nothin' but a low-class asshole no matter what you
ever might fukkin do. To them, you're always just a po-ass little
peckerwood. So, there ain't no way to win. The sumbiches
gotcha. They got you nailed forever inside that gotdamn im-
movable hairdo of theirs. And you ain't ever get'n out, 'cause
they just pull it tighter and tighter till their fukkin eyes slant, and
they make sure there ain't nowhere you can go, since, of course,
you ain't come from nothin' and you don't talk right, and your
ears are too fukkin big and stick out, so that no matter what you

dress up in, you'll always look like a fukkin redneck; and, even if you was to become president or turn out to be Jesus Fukkin Chreyest hissef, a woman like that would still look at you with that little stuck-up smile that says "Keep wigglin', muthafukka. It ain't no use, 'cause you ain't never gon' be anything more than what I got you pegged as."

What if I *was* a dumbass sunavabitch? How is that supposed to make me any different from half the muthafukkas in the world? It don't. Plus, the other half of the assholes on earth is just as dumb; I guess it's just that they ain't sunavabitches—and that's the only fukkin difference I can see. Me, though, I don't mind bein' dumb *and* bein' a sunavabitch. For one thing, I find a helluva lot of peace in bein' a sunavabitch. A sunavabitch don't have to worry about nothin', and I guess that's why I really never have. Plus, *as* a sunavabitch, I seem to always give another sumbich his due, meanin' that I do not low-rate his ass the way other people have a tendency to.

And that's all I got to say about Miss Florence. Well, hell, she's dead now anyhow, so fukher. That's my motto. But I will say this: if I had been the last man on earth and she was the last woman, I guaran-dam-tee you there wouldna been no new people.

Anyway, I told her about the submarine. And what happened was she actually believed me and Voyd, and she called up Mr. Brainsong down at the high school—that's your mama's brother—to come up to the Sheriff's office to hear more about it.

Well, after we done described it as best we could, he set there and didn't say nothin' for a while, just puffed on that fukkin pipe of his that always seemed like it needed to be lit again and smelled like a room full of blue-haired old women. Then he said that he b'lieved he knowed for sure it weren't no American submarine and that, from what we told him, it sounded an awful lot like a German U-boat called a Type 1A, which didn't mean shit to me and Voyd.

Anyway, he knew all about the subject because he had been in the Navy during the war, and submarines was his hobby or some such doo-wah as that. If you ast me, the sumbich—your uncle, I mean—musta spent his *en*tire life underwater. The story was he had his dick shot off. I don't know about that, but he did wear bow ties, and they wuddn nem clip-on kind, neither—which I can't say the same for them Mohammedans, but I'll get back to them later.

Anyway, he said there had been a fair amount of ships that got sank down on the Gulf Coast back in the war and that it was known that at least one of them German submarines had come up into the Mississippi River around 1942. Hell, I bet the muthafukkas went to New Orleans and had a good time. I know I would. Anyway, he said that if they'da come in when the water was high, they coulda gone up it a long fukkin way and not been noticed, if they'da done right, and he 'spect they would have, bein' Germans and all.

He said there woulda been lots of problems, but he figured they coulda done it, as, in-fukkin-deed, it "appeared they had." But, when he ast us where exactly the submarine was, that's when my ass puckered, because I flat out didn't know, and neither did Voyd. Hell, we was lost. If I'da knowed where the submarine was when we was there, we wouldna been lost, but we was. 'Course I couldn't come right out and admit to that, and it was that kinda holdin' back on what we was sayin' that made him think somethin' was funny. And when we said we wuddn sure we could find it again, he allowed he thought that was kinda strange; and then Miss Florence, she begin to apologize, sayin' she had no idea we didn't know where the fuk the thing was and that she was so sorry she'd done got him to come all the way

down to the office and all that—and I thought "all the way?,"
what's that, four fukkin feet, in a little old town like St. Leo?

Well, he didn't seem *too* put out about it, and, in fact, he
said to her that he had *no doubt* that we had *probably* seen a
German-fukkin-submarine because we had described it, as he
put it, "exceedingly well" and that the average person could not
make up something like that. It was what we said about the
cables and what we seen up in the tall part that let him know we
was tellin' the truth. And Voyd said, "Fukkin-A!" At which Miss
Florence looked like a blue racer had just run up her butt.

6

How the Submarine Provides the Clue to Shaw's Hideout — Jack Smiley's Crop Duster — Me and Voyd Shoot Up the Silo

WE TOLD HIM WE WOULD *TRY* TO HELP HIM LOCATE IT, AND then we all agreed not to say nothin' more about it until we did, and when we ast him what happened to the coksukkas who run it up the river, he said that "in all likelihood" they was still here—or, he said, somewhere in America. That bore out my idea, and I figured they really was livin' right here in Mississippi. Why the fuk would they want to go anywhere else?—well, with the possible exception of New Orleans. But I must admit I didn't see no future for 'em in Meffis.

Well, fuk yeah, I know they was the *enemy*, but it's just hard to think of white people bein' your enemy, and from what I understand, them Germans is mostly white.

I am now a clever, small animal on the run from killers. I feel their footsteps in the pounding of my heart. I hear their voices as they go by, searching for me, and I can say "Don't shoot!" in German.

But, perhaps, it occurs to me,

being lost is being alive, at least in my case.
I shall hold that thought, like water in the hand,
which runs away, falls into the earth,
rises, and comes back again as rain and snow
to wash away my shape and cover me over
till I am water too.

All of that is far beyond my ability to understand it, though I have no trouble whatsoever in believing it. After all, if understanding were essential to belief, more people would fish on Sunday.

YOU REMEMBER I TOLD YOU about the "Sledge" woman? Now she's got me goin' to church somewhat more'n I might want to. And the other week she was upset because I didn't get up and go down front to accept Jesus Chr*eye*st as my personal savior. Plus, she was naggin' my ass about me not standin' up and testifyin' for the Lord, or some such shit as that, but I told her I wuddn *about* to stand up there in church and tell the whole fukkin room all the shit I done in the last sixty years. Fukkum. Not unless they tell me what they done, and so far I ain't heard nothin' you'd want to set your hair on fire about.

Anyway, I ast her, "Why are you off onto all this shit?" And she said, "I want to be sure you're saved."

"Saved for what?" I ast her.

And she said, "Why, Junior Ray, you got to be saved so you can enter the kingdom of heaven!"

"Fuk that shit," I told her. "I'm doin' pretty good just to be goin' to church in the first place and hang my ass in there on them gotdamn sawhorses once a fukkin week on Sunday just for an hour and fifteen minutes. So I know I couldn't stand no e-fukkin-ternity of that crap, even if, as I have said before, some of

them sermons the preacher preaches is pretty inter-restin'."
Then I ast her what she thought was goin' to go on up there in
heaven, and she started flappin her mouth about how we'd be
part of the heavenly hosts and would sing praises *un*to the Lord
forever. Well, fuk that.

I can't speak for nobody else, but I know that praisin'
bullshit don't appeal to me, and, to tell the truth, I happen to
know she really don't think much of it neither, which is why I
can't understand why she's so hipped on the fukkin subject; so
I figured I'd just have to ast her the sixty-fukkin-four-dollar
question. So I said, "Well, gotdamnit, if we was in heaven,
would Miz Squint get to shake hands with Mr. Floppy again?"

She had to think about that one for a second or two, and
when she didn't say nothin', I said, "Why don't you just ast that
coksukkin' preacher what the fuk Miz Squint and Mr. Floppy
can do up there?" And then I added, "Speakin' for Mr. Floppy,
I think eternity is a long-ass time for that Buick-size pussy of
yours to go without a tune-up." And she got pissed off and told
me I wuddn very spiritual, and I said, "Kiss my rusty fukkin ass.
I'm as spiritual a muthafukka as you'll ever get to know, and
don't you forget it."

Well, she got that gotdamn hurt-dog look on her face and
stuck her lip out and ast me if I thought Miz Squint and Mr.
Floppy could shake hands and make up. I said hell yeah as long
as she would quit talkin' about all that heaven shit, 'cause, I said,
"Mr. Floppy ain't goin' nowhere he ain't welcome."

I ain't kid'n, you got to let these women know who's in
fukkin charge, or them preachers will be runnin' your life. Hell,
women don't know shit. And why they think a preacher knows
a *gotdamn* thing is beyond me. Chr*ey*est, they'd suck his dick if
he told 'em it was the key to the Pearly Gates. The truth is, I
think that probably goes on a lot, especially with some nem

young sumbiches up in the hills, way off the road back in nem lil' ol' holy-roller churches. Well, it's probably pretty hard on preachers, too, with all them women want'n to cook him a chicken—'cause, if he's got any sense, he knows damn good and well if he lets 'em do it too much, he'll wind up cookin' his own fukkin goose. Kiss my leg.

Well, back to what I was talkin' about. Bone Face and his niggas run us around real good. But that was all right. I eventually got to the right place, even if it didn't work out the way I wanted it to. And the way I got there was by lookin' for where the submarine was, so Voyd and me could tell Mr. Brainsong so him and his friends could get back in there and take a fukkin look at it.

This was the reason I got hold of Jack Smiley and made him to ride me around in his crop duster. He didn't want to do it, but I had somethin' on him he didn't want his wife to know. Hell, I wuddn a deputy sheriff for nothin'. 'Fore it was over I had somethin' on a whole mess of folks. The trouble is that most of the time there wuddn never nothin' I ever seemed to need that would have made bringin' it up worth it. I mean, just because I mighta seen some asshole parked out over cross the levee doin' it with a telephone operator don't necessarily get you no-where—except when one of 'em got elected mayor; then I knew my job was safe for a while, and after that I got a Chevy pickup half-price from another sumbich who knowed I seen him and one of the girls who worked out at the Boll and Bloom comin' out of the Ditty Wah Ditty Tourist Court up on Highway 51 on the way into Meffis. I guaran-fukkin-tee you there wuddn never no tourists there—who the fuk in his right mind woulda thought about bein' a tourist in Meffis, Tennessee!—'course that was before Elvis and all that shit. A lot of times it was best to cut off of 61 onto Brooks Road and go over to 51. Well, hell,

they's a whole fukkin science about how to get in and out of
Meffis if you live in the Delta.

Anyway, Jack Smiley had one nem big old yellow Steerman
double-wing things, and he put me in the poison hopper, which
used to be the front seat. Bear in mind, too, that it was in the
dead of winter, and I had to hold on like a muthafukka 'cause
they wuddn no seat belts, and if he'da turned upside down, I'da
fell out. Plus, I didn't think about that till it was too late and we
was already up in the air, and then I thought, "Oh, shit!" And I
think he musta thought about it, too, 'cause I seen him lookin'
at me a couple of times with a real crazy look in his eye. 'Course,
if it hadda been me flyin' the plane, and he'da been me, I'da
dumped his ass in a blue minute.

But he's too nice, if you know what I mean. He was one nem
fukkas that felt guilty about commit'n a sin and all that shit.
Fukkim. I shoulda told his wife anyway. But she was ugly
enough to marry a bear, and me just thinkin' about him havin'
to deal with that on a daily basis was enough to satisfy the whim.
What it was though was I caught him whippin' off in his car at
cheerleader practice. That woulda gone over like a turd in a
punch bowl.

I noticed him bouncin' up and down in the front seat and
thought it looked mighty fukkin funny, him just bouncin' up
and down like that all by hissef, so I walked up from behind, and
there he was, chokin' the old chicken—he tried to hide it under
a buncha old check books and invoices and shit like that, but
none of that would stay put, so his whacker just popped right up
out of it like some kinda little mushroom just set'n there in his
lap.

I didn't say nothin', and he didn't say nothin'. But he
knowed I saw it and that I knew what was goin' on. Some years
later the Meffis police caught him at it up there parked near one

nem Catholic girls' schools, after school, when them sweet little Catholics was walkin' home. He told the judge there was somethin' wrong with his zipper. They didn't do much to him, except the judge said if they ever caught him for anything *at all* in Meffis, again, he was gonna go to jail. Plus, some nem lil' ol' gals' daddies was in the court room, so I truly believe Jack never did go back up there, and I reckon he musta been awful lonesome after that.

Smiley and me flew all over the place. Except for the fact that he coulda th'owed me out, I had mysef a helluva time, and I learned that there's more'n one way to look at a thing. Shoot, everything was different down on the ground. And I could see it all together in a way I hadn't never thought of before. I even liked the cold—Smiley give me one nem big old airforce parkers and some goggles, and shit I was fixed up.

Plus, in no time at all we found the submarine. Well, hell, we flew out over the Hawk Lake woods, and, with all the leaves gone, it wuddn two minutes and I was lookin' right down on it. I pointed it out to Smiley, and I could see his mouth say "holy shit," and he give me a thumbs-up; so, right there, I knew he wuddn gonna th'ow me outa the plane after that. You just don't give a sumbich the thumbs-up sign and then th'ow his ass out of a fukkin airplane—even I wouldna done that, bearin' in mind there ain't a lot I wouldn't do—and I might add, by God, ain't done. So I felt better about the whole thing. I even wished I coulda said, "Jack, I never saw you bouncin' around skinnin' your stick that day in the car," but that wouldna made no sense, so I just let it alone. Fukkit.

At first I wondered why nobody had ever spotted that submarine from the air before, and then I realized why. Fuk, nobody was ever lookin' for it. I don't 'spec many hunters ever even went back in there. They mostly liked to stay near the log'

road 'cause they were scared they'd get lost—just like Voyd and
me. See, down here in the Delta, there ain't no landmarks. And
if it gets dark, unless you can find yourse'f a troop of Boy
Sprouts—you can forget it. Plus, nobody ever flew over the
place much, and if they'da done it in the spring and summer,
they still might notta seen it even if they was lookin' for it,
'cause, when it's warm, that's a fukkin jungle down there. Even
the animals get lost.

'Course, I hate to say it, but a lotta that's changed now.
These days you got a different kinda turkey out here, and the
muthafukka is playin' poker and shoot'n craps in the casinos,
built on the wet side of the levee where before there was a few
cotton fields but mostly just wildness—dark, swallow–your–
ass–up wildness. 'Course, all that is a good twenty miles north
of where I'm talking about, but still . . . Back to what I was
sayin', though, it was by goin' up in the air with Jack Smiley and
lookin' for the submarine that I got my first big clue to where
Leland Shaw really was, because just before him and me took off
from the little dirt strip there on the side of the highway south
of St. Leo, he said if I didn't mind he needed to fly in the other
direction, out towards the Yellow Dog, so he could check out a
piece of land he was gonna have to dust later on in the year, and
I said fuk yeah I didn't give a shit one way or the other. So when
we took off I got to see what the lay of the land was like out east,
between Highway 61 and the Dog and all around Little Texas,
where I had growed up, well, for a while anyway, after we got
here from over around Clay City in the hills. But fuk all that
noise. Here's what I saw.

I saw the fukkin shadow of a road that wuddn no road. And
I knew it was the old trail I had heard Lawyer Montgomery talk
about. I have to admit that, even though he didn't have no time
for a sumbich like me, I liked him a hell of a lot. He was a real

interestin' fella—always had a buncha rocks in his pocket, and one time told me one of 'em was a piece of a star, and I said "Holy Fukkin Shit!," which, I guess musta kinda put him off somewhat, 'cause he walked on and didn't say nothin'. Anyhow, I never did forget the things he told me, and, in a way, I wished I coulda heard him say more, but he was always busy with them planters in his little law office across the street from the court-house, and I was workin' for Sheriff Holston and busy down in the alley behind the stores with the niggas, so we just didn't cross one another's tracks that much, except when one nem planters needed to get one of his niggas outa jail so he could get his fukkin cotton crop planted. It was like a seesaw. You can see the other person, and you're both more or less doin' the same thing, but you're always goin' in different directions, and there's a lotta space in between.

Anyway, Jack Smiley and me flew over the field that old silo was in, and that's when I saw the fukkin evidence. All out right around the silo was a lot of litter—bread sacks, candy wrappers, old empty Double Cola bottles, and all kinds of shit like that, which I knew was out of place, for one thing, because it was the middle of the fukkin winter, and weren't nobody workin' in the fields, and for another thing because I also seen a buncha tracks—even though the ground was mostly hard as a preacher's dick, I could still see them footprints all over the place, where they had flattened out the dry grass, and where they was busted through little patches of ice between the rows in the field. Plus, they was goin' in mostly only two directions: one, to the gravel road that run alongside the field, and two, over towards the shadow of that old trail where they just stopped once't they got up to it, just like they did when they got to the gravel in the other direction.

Well, about the gravel, I could understand. But, now, the

part about 'em stoppin at the old trace, I ain't never figured that out.

However, there was no gotdamn mistakin' that somebody had been comin and goin' back and fukkin forth to that silo, and I mean right up to where the chute was, too. Plus, after I was back on the ground, I later saw that those tracks was a lot less noticeable when you was on the ground, which is why, if I hadn't never gone up in that crop duster with Jack Smiley to look for that fukkin submarine, I wouldna known to this day that Leland Shaw had been holed up inside that silo. And Voyd and me would've run ourselves ragged chasin' left handed monkeywrenches out around the levee and God knows where the fuk else.

That gotdamn Bone Face would've had us runnin all the way to De-fukkin-troit if the whole thing had kept up any longer than it did. That's where all the niggas used to go in them days, De-troit. I ain't never been there, and I ain't never goin' because I know I'll just see ever' fukkin black bastud I ever knew and had to th'ow in jail on Satuday night back yonder down in St. Leo. And I don't think that would be too good for me. Well, fuk the sumbiches. I'm glad they're gone. 'Course the more of 'em that left, the less it was for me to do, and that, plus my age, is one reason I ain't a deputy no more—although, in a manner of speaking, I am still in law enforcement.

Anyhow, after that plane ride, I got hold of Voyd, and me and him went out to the silo. We leaned up against the patrol car for a while, and just looked at it to see if we could tell if there was anybody up in it. Well, we couldn't, so we shot at it.

And we had us a time, too! I had brung along the .30-caliber, water-cooled machine gun, and a tripod that belonged to the Sheriff's office—it had been there since what Sheriff Holston called the "last war," and nobody had ever shot the thing. Hell, it just sat up there in the dadgum anteroom, locked up, and I didn't see no sense in not taking it out and testin' it. There weren't never gon' be no gotdamn riots in St. Leo nohow—what would they have been about, integratin' the Boll and Bloom Cafe? Shee-it. So I said fukkit and grabbed up the gun and then went back in and toted out a whole chest full of ammunition. They was all tracers, too—well, every fifth one on the belt anyway. And that's what made it the most fun of all.

Me and Voyd got so caught up in playin' with the machine gun that we damn near forgot about why we was out there. It was a show.

There wuddn nobody around, just me and Voyd, and it was get'n late in the afternoon, so that made the whole thing that much better, because it allowed the tracers to stand out more'n they would have otherwise if it had been the middle of the day. It was like squirt'n fire out the end of your finger.

We set it up on the ground on the edge of the field. It was not hard to figure out how to load it, especially since I had read about the proper procedure in a magazine. Well, I say *read* about it; I looked at some pictures, but it amounted to the same fukkin thing—bein' in law enforcement I felt like I needed to know that kinda stuff, so, short of havin' actually shot one, I guess I knew pretty much enough about it to get it started. And I did put water in the sumbich. Voyd had a' Arkansas credit card, and we siphoned some out of the radiator of the patrol car into that fat-ass thing around the barrel of the gun.

After that, we shot and shot that muthafukka until we couldn't shoot it no more 'cause we had done shot up all them belts of cart'iges. I guess if a person hadn't never seen nothin' like that they couldn't know what it was like, unless they had watched the I-raqi war on CNN and seen all them tracers goin' up in the air, on the TV. Well, it was like that only not at night, plus I don't reckon we was shoot'n the same things them I-raqis was, but the way it looked was similar.

And it was fukkin impossible to miss. All I had to do was point it and, just like I was aiming a stream of water, hose down whatever I was shoot'n at; only it was with lead. I could see wherever it hit, even without the tracers, but the tracers let me see where them slugs went *after* they hit because them boogers hit that silo and skinnied way-ass straight up in the air and ricocheted full fukkin force every whichaway off to the side and, I mean, son, flat *tore up* that silo. Concrete was poppin off all over the place, and when we got through, which was when we had done shot up all the cart'iges, the silo looked like somebody had just beat the shit out of it with a fukkin sledge hammer. It looked like your dick would if it was a corn cob.

The ground was covered in empty brass cart'ige casings; the silo didn't look nothin' like it did before we shot it up, and somethin' was wrong with the fukkin gun: the barrel was bent. I guess we didn't put enough water in the sumbich. And that's when Voyd said, "Oh, shit, Junior Ray."

"Oh, shit, what, Voyd?" I said.

"Looky yonder what we done," he said. And I didn't say nothin' for a minute because I guess it just hadn't sank in what it was he was talkin' about, so I said, "What in the gotdamn dog-fuk are you talkin' about, Voyd?" And he says, "Junior Ray, how the gotdamn hell are you goin' to explain what you done to that thing?"—and he pointed to the silo.

"Fuk the silo," I said. "I don't have to explain nothin'—and what's all this *'you'* shit? You done it, too, you little piss-ant."

And he said, "Now, I don't know, Junior Ray, I wuz just tryin' to hep *yew* han'l your equipment so you could find the maniac. I didn't know you wuz gonna fuk up the silo."

You have to understand how Voyd thinks in order to catch

on to what the fuk he's tryin' to say. Ev'ry since we was in high school and got in trouble once't, Voyd has tried to capitalize on the notion that he is a person "who is easily led." Which is why he ain't ever amounted to much, and if it hadn't of been for him marryin' Sunflower, he wouldna amounted to nothin' at all. The little sumbich loves to have a good time but don't ever want to claim he's had nothin' to do with whatever it is he's had a good time doin'. They's a lot of muthafukkas like that.

Anyway, then I realized what he was drivin' at. The silo belonged to Miss Helena Ferry, and, even though she wuddn very likely to ever come out there and take a look at it, some of them niggas—or one of them planters—was gonna tell her what the thing looked like and probably who did it, 'cause I realized, too, that it was just possible that all the time we was havin' ourselves a ball with that machine gun, one of Bone Face's niggas coulda been off somewhere watchin' the whole thing and probably was, but in the excitement of it all, I just didn't stop to think about nothin' but what I was doin', which I fukkin admit is a shortcoming of mine, not that I give a shit; but, anyway, the point is that, even though that old silo hadn't been used in thirty years or more, it was still *her property,* and fukkin with somebody's property in that day and time—and even now—down here in the Delta was like rape or some such shit as that, or, to tell the truth, worse. Hell, a man might shoot you and cut your nuts off for messin' with his woman; but, when it come to property, he would shoot you, cut your nuts off and *then* make you stick 'em in your mouth just for fukkin' with his land, even if you was already dead. So, potentially, I was in a tight spot.

Just because Miss Helena was a woman didn't mean she couldn't raise hell about it. And Sheriff Holston woulda knowed in a blue minute who had done it if he'd 'a been called out there and seen all them spent cart'iges layin' all over the fukkin ground. So the question was what was I gonna do, and what was I gonna say if I had to say anything.

For starters, I knew I could turn it around on Voyd, if I had to, and say that he had done brung the gun out there and that I had looked for his ass all over the county and that when I finally found him he had done done the damage, shot up all the ammunition, and fukked up the gun. I could've done that if I had had to, and I would have.

He'd a' jumped up and down and denied he done it, but Voyd had already told so many lies nobody around back then woulda believed him. It wasn't simply that he didn't have no credibility. Later on that might have been restored. But that wasn't the case with Voyd. Going back to his earliest days, as far as most people were concerned, it was more like he had done shit in the well of truth. So, he would not have had a fukkin prayer.

He woulda got over it, and if he didn't ever, then fukkim. I'd 'a just had myself one less friend, that's all. But I'da kept my job, and, at the time, that was the only thing that mattered, mainly because I truly thought that by remainin' a deputy I still had a chance of bein' able to kill that fukkin Leland Shaw and not have to answer for it. Anyway, that was my plan. I couldn't see no other way.

It was one thing to shoot tracers at a concrete tower full of old cotton seeds and a lunatic, but it was somethin' else to do what I had in mind, and I was bent on doin' it. Why? 'Cause I just fukkin *wanted* to, that's why. I was tired of killin' small stuff—turtles and snakes, dogs, and birds on the electric wire. That wuddn enough no more, and somethin' was just drivin' my ass to shoot somethin' that had a little more meat on it, in a manner of speakin'. It's hard to explain, because I don't know if I ever fully understood it mysef. All I know is turkeys and deer didn't count, that was hunt'n. Killin' a man, though, seemed like there was somethin' what you might call *basic* about it. And the need to get it done it was almost more than I could stand. The question was how to do it in the line of duty.

How beautiful alienation is! What a sense of identity – identity in its purest, most incontrovertible form, in fact! Indeed, I am so attracted at times that I almost cease to care if I get home again, and I really feel I could become quite happy in this tower for the rest of my life, except, of course, when those persistent Saxons are shooting at it. The rifles don't bother me, but, I must admit, the machine gun was very disturbing, and I thought there was a chance one or two of the rounds might find their way inside. If any have, they must have come in lower. I do not understand why the soldiers never actually attack.

Perhaps it is because of the watchmen. I see them all the time. They stand and watch. They are not looking for me, because I believe they know precisely where I am hiding, and so I have come to feel safe when they are nearby.

These watchmen
have dark skins and
remind me of Negroes.
That, in itself,
is a source of considerable comfort.

THEN, SURE ENOUGH, AFTER VOYD AND ME had crawled around all over the gotdamn ground and picked up as many of them empty cart'iges and other little doodads, like them pieces of the belts they was stuck in, sure e-fukkin-nough, right as we was leavin' here come a couple of nigga rabbit hunters, and we said, "Hi yawl," and they said, "Yassuh, Cap'm, yassuh, hi yawl doin'?" And we said, "What the fuk yawl huntin' outchee-uh this time of night?" And they said, "Aw, Mis' Junior, we ain't hunt'n. We lookin' fo' our dog."

Fuk. They didn't have no dog. We woulda seen it. We knowed exactly what they was up to. When you see two niggas walkin' around at night with a couple of double-barrel shotguns, they ain't lookin for no muthafukkin' dawg. Those coksukkas was lookin' for *us*.

So I said, "Yawl boys better get on home, now, you hear?"

And they said, "Yassuh, Cap'm, yassuh, Cap'm pleez! We goin' there now." You know how they do, with all that yassuh shit and laughin' and slappin' their leg and lookin' like all they ever want to do is make you the happiest sumbich in the world, when you know gotdamn good and well they hate your ass and that, instead of a rabbit's foot in their pocket, they would rather be carryin' around *your* fukkin foot. Well, I guess, when you think of it, that would make 'em feel pretty gotdamn lucky.

But all that's in the past. The world's different now. Of course, *I'm* not. I didn't have nothin' to change to.

But here's the thing, and if I'm lyin', I'm dyin'. I seen him. I know I seen him.

It was dark, but it was that part of the dark that ain't quite pitch black yet, and I seen him out of the corner of my eye. I was lookin' off down the road and not at the silo when, right on the edge of my eyeball I seen a dark lump kind of fall out of the chute and hit the ground for just a split second, and then it moved off, away from the base of the silo; and when I looked over towards it, it wuddn nothin' there. It was gone. And by that time everything was plumb dark. But I know it was him. It fukkin had to be. I seen it with my gotdamn cone cells.

I told Voyd to look, and he said he didn't never see nothin'. But, somehow, I never expected he would.

Shaw had been up in that silo the whole time we was shoot'n that machine gun. Now, I only saw a lump of darkness, but I will go to my fukkin grave believin' it was that crazy sumbich. And, fuk, there was somethin' dark about him to begin with. It was like the Devil was callin' all the shots in my whole life back in them days.

Now the question is why didn't we just go get the volunteers and go up inside that silo that very night—or at least the very next day? The answer to that is at the time I just wasn't sure I had seen anything. It didn't really sink in until much later. And, of course, we did go up in there, and we did find where he had been holed up in there, and that's where I found them notebooks, which as you already know are weirder than a hoop skirt on a halfback.

Plus, it took some doin' to get anybody to go up the chute and look inside that silo. I sure as hell wuddn gonna do it, and Voyd wuddn gon' be the first either. Finally, we made that dumb sumbitch T-Bone Clack go up in there. He was so fat it was hard for him to get up the chute, and he was scared a little, plus he was huffin' and puffin' so much I thought he was gonna have a fukkin heart attack—he did have one a few years later at an Ole Miss football game over at Oxford.

Somebody got him some seats down near the fifty-yard line, and, when the Rebel band marched out at half-time and all them twirlers started jumpin' around right there in front of him, well, I guess, bein' a strict Baptist, all them high-flyin' thighs and snappy little crotches was just too much for him. It seems he just kept bendin' over and bendin over, sort of sideways in his seat, and the people behind him got upset because they thought he was just tryin' to look up under the majorettes' little skirts. And then these same people got pissed when he didn't stand up for the kick-off.

But, of course, he couldn't—because he was dead. Well, it didn't matter anyway, 'cause T-Bone never did give a shit about football.

    . . . . One life may be no more significant than the flight of a distant bird across our line of sight, appearing for a moment, occupying space and being part of the world we see, then disappearing and leaving all we view without a trace of its having passed – not a tree, not a cloud, nor a building altered by either the presence or the absence of the bird. That is what one life of one man may be like. I was thinking about my father though not as an analog to the bird. . . .

7

Niggas, Planters, & Bankers — Miss Helena's House — Revolving Mohammedans — A Pussy Bomb — We Go Inside the Silo

VOYD IS LIKE A DOG. HE THINKS SPIT IS THE ANSWER TO everything. He spits on his shoes to make 'em shine. He spits on the stock of his shotgun to make it shine. He spits on his fukkin hands before he grabs a hold of anything. He spits on the gotdamn windshield when he wants to clean it off, and, according to what he told me back yonder, he used to spit on his dick before he poked it in Sunflower—or she did; I forget which. Anyway, for Voyd, spit is a way of life.

Well, I don't know why I brought it up—it's just that whenever I think of Voyd, I think about how he spits on ever'thing. I mean, it don't have nothin' directly to do with anything we ever did, but I guess from time to time I have to sort of freshen up my view of Voyd, because the past is beginning to have a tendency to fade out a little, and I don't want to lose it. If I did, that'd be the fukkin end of me.

Hell, me and the past is the same thing. I'm just it in human form, and when they bury me, well, they'll be coverin' up a footprint in the backyard of history. But that's all right. What's past was all based on dirt to begin with, and that's where it ought to go—if, with all this buildin' and pavin', they's any dirt left to dig a fukkin hole in. Chr*ey*est, they got four-lane highways runnin' out through the beanfields now, takin' all these outa-town sumbiches to the casinos 'cross the levee.

Spring always arrived in the middle of winter, usually in February, and snakes came out to lie in the warm dirt of the road. Flowers, too, rose up and bloomed only to be blasted once again by darkness and ice. Nevertheless, there in February, people sweated and, afterwards, caught cold.... And, then, the later greening, soft, light at first like the mist of an imaginary gas, grew more visible, fecund in the warming, wetness of the earth, while, across the levee, the river swelled, swift, obese, and angry, engorged on the melting of a nation, the water, like a living beast, violent and spreading, reaching Amazonic into Arkansas.

And fish invaded the forests on both sides, to be shot with pistols, netted, or speared with gigs – huge carp and giant buffalo, tough, coarse, full of bones and as big as a leg but edible and enjoyed by those less fortunate who could not afford flounder from the Coast. And there were gar: alligator gar, atavistic and long – ten, eleven, twenty-two feet – which came up out of the lashing waves and Mississippi whirlpools to eat anything and all that their toothy, Devonian snouts could swallow. They broke the lines, straightened the hooks, ate the nets, and, some say, drank the flood away.

TOWARD THE END OF IT ALL, I noticed Atlanta Birmin'-fukkin-ham Jackson and them four big Mohammedan muthafukkas she had in tow riding around all over the county. I mean, when you're a deputy sheriff in a small Mississippi Delta county, that kind of shit is easy to notice.

What I didn't know was what they was up to—I do now, because over the years I have found it out and pieced it together, but then I didn't know what the fuk was really goin' on. But I did know, maybe just through instinct, that seein' them around had somethin' to do with that gotdamn Leland Shaw. And I guess I knew, too, that they was out to get him before I could. It's too bad a man has to know all the important shit in his life thirty years after it could have made some difference.

And then, right there at the time just before Sheriff Holston come and told me to not do no more about tryin' to locate the mainiac, Atlanta B. Jackson and them four Mohammedan muthafukkas—and Bone Face, *and* that gotdamn Milton Casequarter—plus Mr. Humes, the banker, along with Lawyer Montgomery and Dr. Austin—Hell, didn't nothin' important ever happen without them two being together. . . and the truth is Sheriff Holston, hissef; though neither him nor any of them other white men was what you might call visible, 'cause they was all off in a back room, and I knowed it but couldn't prove it, well, but the fact is ever' one of them sumbiches was *all* over at Miss Helena's house.

Bear in mind I ain't sayin' Sheriff Holston was a sumbich 'cause he wuddn. But he was there just the same, even though he would claim he was not and never had nothin' to do with none of that stuff. But that's how them planters is—planters and niggas, they's all the same if you ast me. Fukkum. Well, all except Sheriff Holston, and I owe him a lot and always will.

Anyway, me and Voyd, not knowin' the whole story at the time, we seen all that goin' on over there. And, too, because we believed Leland Shaw was with them niggas and was hide'n inside his aunt Miss Helena Ferry's house, we further believed it was our duty to go in there and get him.

That was a fukkin mistake. He *was* in there, but there

weren't no way on this earth Voyd and me was ever gonna get in there to pin it down.

I guess, too, I knew right then that I wasn't going to get to shoot his ass, but I still had to make out like I was actin' in the public-fukkin-interest, which I, frankly, never really have, but that's beside the point. So I was gonna take him into custody and more or less turn him over to Sheriff Holston, which, it turns out, I wouldn't have had to do in the first place.

When Voyd and me got to the house, we parked the patrol car beside that big ass black limousine with the Land-of-Lincoln license plates and walked up on the porch and rung the bell. The door opened and here was them four big Chicago-nigga bucks, ever' one of 'em in a suit and a bow tie standin' there one right behind the other, and the one in front had his hands behind him, which I noticed but didn't understand why until later. And I said, "Move outa the way, you black bastud, and let me in." And he, the one standin' in the front of the line, said, "Yassuh," and moved outa the way, but the next one behind him took his place and stood there lookin' straight at me, with his hands behind his back, and not movin', and I said, "Listen, you blue-gum uppity muthafukka, I said move your dumb sef outa the fukkin way!" And then that one, just as polite as you please, said, "Yassuh," and moved outa the way and went on back and stood at the end of the line like the last one, and so there I was lookin' at a third one; and ever'time I said move outa the way, they'd say "Yassuh" and go to the back of the line, and another one nem Mohammedan sumbiches would take his place. I near 'bout lost my fukkin mind.

Well, Voyd, that stupid coksukka, put his hand on his pistol; and, the instant he did, I heard a hammer cock back right in front of me behind that black muthafukka's back, and then, a split second later, I heard three more hammers click back, and that's when I noticed all four of them muthafukkas had their hands behind their backs, so I knowed then that the one at the front had had a pistol behind him all the time and that, when he'd say "Yassuh" and go to the back of the line, he'd just hand the piece off to the sumbich standing behind him, and then that one would stick it behind *his* back and so on; plus, when I heard *all* them other hammers cock back, that just proved all four of them muthafukkas had been tote'n guns in their pockets to begin with. It didn't surprise me none. Actually, I'da thought it was pretty funny if they hadn't been. But I ain't yet figured out why they was all revolvers. Bein' niggas, don't you know, seems like they'da been carry'n them little automatics.

Anyway, sometimes bein' white don't mean a thing. So I said, to them four *revolvers*, "Aw-ight, since you boys done what I ast yawl, I-mo let yawl off easy. Go on back in there, and do whatever Miss Helena tells yawl to—and I don't want to have to come back here, you hear?"

And they said, "Yassuh," and shut the fukkin door. But, now, what could I do? They had done did what I ast 'em if you wanta get technical about it; plus, at the time, I seen Miss Helena back up in the house lookin' straight at me, and I knowed she knowed what was goin' on, so I knowed I didn't stand a Chinaman's chance of get'n inside, and I guess that her lookin' at me thatta way was what let me know the whole thing was over; only I didn't know just how. In other words, I knew, I guess, that me get'n a-hold of Leland Shaw was no longer a possibility and that I was not going to be able to do what I had intended, namely to blow his ass off. And that, naturally, was a big disappointment. But I was up against more that just some crazy, runaway, shell-shocked sumbich that, as far as I was concerned, needed to be shot. (And, if I'da had my way, I'da had the muthafukka stuffed. I ain't kidd'n.) Anyway, what I was really up against was all *them* versus me. Only nobody was ever gonna say it. And I wuddn neither.

Of course, all that was more or less right when Voyd and me and some of the volunteers was planning to blow up the silo, which we never did do, although it woulda been a helluva show. But I'm glad we didn't go through with it even though I doubt there would have been a whole lot said about it later—not even by Miss Helena, whose silo it was. My guess is at the time she was just satisfied enough that she had got her way about Leland Shaw, and that was all that mattered to her. Plus, and I say this now that I think back on it, I believe she was slippin', if you know what I mean. I believe she was beginning to get fukkin senile—because it wuddn too many years after all that that she lost ever' piece of property she owned and wound up on SSI in the the nursin' home down in Clarksdale, 'cause she was declared a pauper.

And it was a good thing, too, on account of she'd have just wound up livin' in a ditch otherwise, 'cause, there in the end, she didn't have two sticks to rub together.

What happened was this: she mortgaged all her property, and the bank would let her have a little draw whenever she needed it, since they had ever-fukkin thing she owned. But interest rates rose, and of course she didn't know what the fuk she was doin' in the first place. Plus, her so-called "financial advisor," who was just some silly sumbich she'd known all her life, either didn't know what he was doin' or else he wanted to make sure the fukkin bank got the property, one or the other. I ain't never figured that out.

Then one day, when Miss Helena sent that thievin' field-hand Queenasheba up to the bank to get some money, the bank sent word back by Queenasheba that they wasn't gonna let her have no more. And then, they say, Miss Helena screamed and fell back on the bed where she lay and hollered till Lawyer Montgomery got her hauled off to the nursin' home. And then I think he went to one, too.

The bank kept some of her property and sold the rest on the courthouse steps. The fukkin justice there, if there is any, is that when the bank finally foreclosed and acquired the town property and all her farm land, too, none of it was worth what it was when they had lent her the money. Later, the president of that particular bank bought some of it for himself, cheap, which I didn't never think was particularly the thing a bank president ought to do, and I expect he might be sorry now that he did it. Well, probably not.

I kept referrin' to "the bank." Actually, they was two of 'em. One had the decency to cut her off and not let her borrow no more from them, but the other one, I reckon, was glad to get it all. I imagine they thought they was really makin' a lick. Well, fukkum. Whatever they got, they got what they deserved, and that wuddn much. Plus, I believe they had more than one or two uneasy moments about the whole mess. Mainly, what they done was not real dignified, if you know what I mean.

I suppose here I am soundin' like I'm taking her side of it, and, in a way, I reckon I am, but that's just because I hate bankers worse'n I hate planters. Hell, I hate bankers worse'n I hate niggas, 'cause, at least, when a nigga steals somethin', he's got a good heart; well, normally anyway. But a banker, he ain't got no coksukkin heart at all. Now, with a nigga, no matter how bad he might be, there's a kind of fukkin humanity that let's you know that even though he stole from you, he don't hate you, and, in fact, he might even like you—not that he ought to, mind you, as mean as me and the rest of them other sumbiches like me has been to him—but a banker, Jesus Christ, that muthafukka has about as much feelin' as a buzz saw—maybe not that much.

I got no fukkin time for 'em. If you ast me, the Klan oughta add 'em to the list and lynch a few.

I ain't goin' back on nothin' I believe in, as a white man and, of course, a fukkin Christian, but I think I made my point. And anybody that don't like it can kiss my ass.

However, I'm get'n off the subject. This thing with Leland Shaw was a very powerful event as far as my life is concerned. I couldn't think of nothin' else. And, it's only lately that something occurred to me, and that is that, maybe, it was the *chasin' around* after that sick sumbich I was cravin' and not necessarily the killin' of him. Don't get me wrong, I wouldna hesi-fukkin-tated one gotdamn minute to squeeze off a clip into that crazy fukka. But, somehow—I don't know, maybe too much time has gone by—somehow it does come to me that it might have been the chase and that it is just that—the fukkin *chase*—I miss the most.

Anyhow, as I have already indicated, runnin' around after him got pretty fantastic at times, but never as fantastic as it was when it come to seein' them tracks just end, ka-whump, right at where that old trace was, which run right by outchonda not far from the silo. I mean it was just as if somethin' reached down and snatched his ass up off the earth, 'cause, like I said, them footprints just ceased, ended, disa-fukkin-peared right out in the middle of nowhere—I'm talkin' about in the very middle of a gotdamn bean field.

There are places, I believe, where one step upon the earth changes every horizon and even brings another sky. I sometimes find an invisible wall which seems to separate the shape of one moment from the next – Where there are fields, suddenly, there is forest, and, in some cases the reverse is true. I am reminded of the little woods near town. I played in it as a child but noticed that the ground beneath the trees was furrowed, and I knew, even at that age, that sometime before the trees, cotton had grown on that small forest's floor.

That took time.

But, of course, everything takes time. It is the amount of time that appears to be the point of main concern. And so I have come to think the spaces of time can be leaped over, just as a couple of yards of ground can be shortened by a jump. How this could happen I cannot say, but I do think it possible, and such a maneuver might explain the sudden change of scenery I perceive when I put my foot on certain paths – or in particular directions that, other than a looming distance, have no discernable track.

BUT BEFORE I GET INTO THAT, there's something I been thinking about. I was listening to a sumbich the other day on the television, and he was talkin' about how we was gonna hafta develop a cheap source of super-powerful energy that would drive everything—ever'thang from cars to electric lights and space ships. Plus he said it had to be safe. Well, I lissened and lissened, and then I realized the dumb muthafukka was overlookin' the most powerful fukkin thing in the world. Everybody thinks it's atomic energy, but I say fuk that—it's pussy.

Hell yeah. Any sumbich past the age of twelve knows it's pussy that runs the fukkin world, and it's always been thatta way. What gets me is how them smart muthafukkas on the television could've overlooked that fact. But I guess the most surprisin' thing is that nobody's ever tried to make a bomb out of the stuff. Boy, I could sure get a bang out of that. That's a joke.

Anyhow, it'd be like one of them bombs that just sort of pops and does away with all the folks but leaves the buildings standin'. That's what a pussy bomb would do. When all the men looked up in the sky and seen this huge-ass, mile-wide cunt comin' after 'em, they'd all drop dead of a heart attack. Pretty slick.

Well, hell, I don't know. I done seen just about ever'thang. Take some of these people that comes down here from Meffis to play all night. You get all kinds, but a lot of 'em is people you know *has* somethin'—probably friends of these planters for all I know. Anyway, you look at the man and the woman, and by the way they act and all, you'd think they probably get dressed to screw—like they has special outfits to do it in. He might have special screwin' slacks, and she might have her special fukkin blouse or some such shit as that, but the point is you just can*not* imagine that they ever get nekkid for anything. Shoot, it's like they might not even have no bodies at all underneath them expensive get-ups. Plus, most of the women is too fukkin skinny to sweat. And their pussy, if they even have one, has got to be just kind of an afterthought.

Me, I like a woman on the big side with one nem beehive hairdos, like that sweet thing I mentioned over around Sledge. Help-me-Jesus! By the way, I know I keep referring to her by her approximate location, but, just for the record, her name is Dinah Flo McKeever. Her husband was that asshole, Lonny McKeever, who run an old store over at Tibbs and farmed on the side, and he wasn't worth a shit at either one. That's why I believe he must have been into some other stuff, too—I ain't ever been surprised at what goes on out in the middle of nowhere—otherwise I don't know how he was able to leave her so well fixed.

However, I don't know that I will ever figure out what was

really goin' on back then in them days when I was chasin' after Leland Shaw. Ever' time I get on to one thing, another question pops up. But I do know this. It was like I had a fukkin disease, and the germs was makin' me want to kill that sumbich. Plus, it never has stopped. I still want to even after all this time. It's like I ain't done on this earth what I was meant to do. I can't explain it. I guess it's kind of a spiritual thing, like somehow, there was supposed to be him and me, and we was supposed to play out something that had been already decided, only, from my point of view, it got sidetracked.

Now, the reason I wanted to kill him ain't complicated. I learned, way back yonder when I was workin' as a deputy for Sheriff Holston that a man's motive for doin' somethin' don't have to be complex in any way. None whatsoever. Most of the time when somebody does somethin' against the law, they do it just 'cause they want to. Even though they may tell theirself they're doin' it for this or that and they may see it as all involved, usually there ain't nothin' more to it than that they just flat out wanted to do whatever it was they did. Well, it was the same with me. I didn't have no real good explainable reason for want'n to kill that crazy Leland Shaw other than I just wanted to do it. Plus, I was hellbent on it—and, I might fukkin add, get'n away with it, too. Goin' to Parchman penitentiary was the last thing on *my* mind.

Some people would probably think I'm lucky I didn't get to put myself in that position. But that's bullshit. Believe me, I'da got away with it. I never worried one minute about that. As it is now, though, I just feel I guess whatchacall *unfulfilled*.

I'm convinced it all really began back when I was littler than a duck's dick, because, back yonder in them days, in the hills, over around Clay City, it seemed like a lot of emphasis was placed on killing. Now, I won't say that was true with the women, but it was with the men, and if you were gonna be a man, then you had to do some killing; and that was mostly game, but it also included livestock—hogs in season and stuff like that—plus whatever you seen set'n by the roadside, like tweety birds, turtles, snakes, house cats, and nigga dogs. Hell, back then, you could shoot anything in a nigga's yard. I'm talkin' about guinea hens, ducks, geese, chickens—it didn't matter none. It was almost the same as if they was wild in the woods and didn't belong to nobody. And the niggas wouldn't say nothin', neither. They'd just stay shut up inside till you was gone. I reckon they was scared and knowed better than to try to do anything about it. By god, them was the days.

Well hell, who wouldna been scared, with a bunch a tow-headed, wild eleven-year-old muthafukkas runnin' around with shotguns shoot'n ever'thing in sight. Fuk, I'da been scared, too; and, though I didn't think of it at the time, I suppose knowing that we could blow up just about anything we wanted to was part of why it was so much fun. But that was then, before things got all fukked up. As far as I'm concerned, the whole gotdamn country's gone to the dogs. And, if you ast me, it was all that civil rights shit.

> The interesting insight here is that time is what I have a problem with. Perhaps, It's not so much that I am lost upon the earth as it is that I am lost among the earth or, somehow, within the sequence of events. If that were true, it would explain a lot.
>
> On the other hand, I don't want to become too suspicious about reality. Yet, I can never manage to pin it down, principally because there seems to be more than just one.

BUT, LET ME GET BACK TO THEM FOOTPRINTS. To this day, I

do not have a satisfactory explanation for it. And even though I seen that them tracks just stopped, I do not believe what Bone Face's boys believed, and that is that the old trace snapped him up.

You see, they, Bone Face's lieutenants, thought that the old trail was connected to the past in more ways than one. It's a buncha bullshit if you ask me, although I can't come up with anything much better. Plus, I will say this: no matter what I may think about a nigga, I will be the first to admit they have a way of knowing things that you might say are not knowable to the average white man. I'm not saying they're smarter than we are. I'm just saying they're closer to some type of natural truth than we are.

Anyway, two of Bone Face's jumpers swore that they seen Shaw run out of the silo and out across the field to the south of it and that they run after him but that, when he got near the middle of it, suddenly they couldn't see him no more, and then they seen where his tracks just ended, like he couldn't have gone nowhere but straight up, only they said that wasn't where he went. They said the old trace took him.

In other words, he went off into the past. I asked them how come they didn't go off into the past too, and they said not everybody would or could, it was just some who could and that generally they was people who was a little touched. They said the Lord always held the gate open for them, so that sometimes they could go back an' forth if they found the right road.

I used to get a funny feeling whenever I got near that old trail. It turns out there were a lot of them trails crossing the country, and in the hills you could really pick them out because the ground was so pressed down on account of all the traffic that had been on them, beginning with the buffalo and shit like that, some say for thousands of years before we got here. But I don't know about none of that. And them preachers get all in a wad when you bring it up.

Fukkum. Even if those niggas were right, I don't think that crazy sumbich Leland Shaw ever knew he had gone back in time. He didn't know where he was to begin with. On the other hand, the past is where he wanted to go, when you think about it, because, as I mentioned earlier, he never did believe he had come back home after the war, and he used to just say, over and over, I want to go home, and he did not mean his mama's house.

Of course, I don't *know* that he was in Miss Helena's house that day when the sheriff and Lawyer Montgomery and all them fukkin Mohammedans was over there, but if he weren't, then I don't know what all the fuss was about. Plus, it wouldn't have ended right then and there the way it did. Hell, I think the sumbich went to Chicago with Atlanta Jackson in that long-ass limousine. And that's where he stayed. I never was able to get the sheriff nor nobody else to verify that, and I guess that's because they was afraid I would find him and shoot him just for the hell of it. I don't know, but that's when my career took a nose-dive and went downhill from then on.

Naturally, as anybody can see, I more or less stayed in law enforcement, and now I'm retired from the sheriff's department. But what I got for retirement wasn't much, so that's why I'm working security in the parking lot out here at the casino. It pays all right, and, as long as I do my job they don't fuk with me.

They took my pistol, though. Well, it was theirs, but I've got my own which they don't know nothin' about, so fukkum. Anyway, I ain't supposed to tote a *roscoe* no more when I'm on duty because I pulled it on some little punk from Meffis who called me a redneck sunavabitch. I told him he was correct on both counts but that I was gonna blow his ass off just for being from Meffis. Well, he was driving too fast around the lot, so I had stopped him, and that's when it started. Anyway, the little prick was *connected*, so the personnel office called me in and said I wouldn't be needing a gun no more because they wanted me to think of myself as an ambassiter of goodwill.

Fuk being an ambassiter. And fuk all that goodwill shit, too. I ain't got no time for it. If I'da wanted to be an ambassiter, I'da got myself a job at the discount club. "May I hep yew?" and all that crap. "Good mawnin', muthafukka. I bet your ass is all out of lawn furniture—how 'bout four or five thousand dog biscuits for that fukked up little hound of yours?—or perhaps a simple bowl of catshit, which I expect he'd prefer."

No, sir. I don't want no part of that goodwill crap. Being an ambassiter never got nobody nothin' as far as I can tell. Hell, you say "ambassiter," I say "shotgun." All that slipping and sliding turns my stomach. I mean stuff like, "Excuse me, sir. May I get past your big fat ass?" Hell, I'd just tell the sumbich, "Get out the way, fool!"

I guess my attitude is pretty easy to understand. Most people feel I need friends, but I've always felt friends needed *me*. And that's it in a fukkin nutshell.

The world's done changed. They ain't no place now for what used to be. What was all right then ain't all right no more, and I guess I was born with one foot in one time and the other in another. Back when I was young you could get away with killing a few every now and then, and it didn't cause much of a stir, especially if they was niggas. Hell, now you not only can't shoot one, you can't even cut your eye at him the wrong way. It ain't the same. One time I could have shot Leland Shaw as a public service and one or two of Bone Face's *go-fers* and no-body would have said anything about it. They would have just accepted it as part of the show, unless, of course, some fukkin Yankee newspaper got hold of it.

Oh well, I've learned that almost nothing is what it seems to be. Last week, for instance, Harmon Cogswell came back to town for a few days and was honored by both the Presbyterian and the Methodist church, on account of his wife was a Methodist, because he had been a war hero, a congressman, a great Christian, and all kinds of other shit, and I just had to think that the last time I saw the sumbich was when we was boy sprouts and he, being a couple of years older, was demonstrating how to fuk a cow, which, during the process, shit all over his shoes and his britches, too. It was pretty fukkin funny, if you ask me.

I'm certain God would forgive him, but I ain't too sure about the USDA.

WE WAS GOING TO BLOW UP THE SILO, but we never did because, just about that time was when Sheriff Holston told me it was all over. And, after that day, I never did see Atlanta Birmingham Jackson and her long black limousine with the four Fruit ever again. It was just like the whole thing had never happened.

However, as you know, we did finally go up inside the silo, and we did confirm that Leland Shaw had been there. Hell, he had a real cozy little nest up in the top of a whole tower full of cotton seeds—why in god's name the thing was full of cotton seeds don't nobody know, but it was, and it was the very thing that enabled that crazy sumbich to survive the winter. That plus all the candy bars, bread, red weenies, and everything else he got from Casequarter's store. Hell, he was, if you'll pardon the expression, in high-fukkin-cotton.

There *was* one other thing I can't get out of my mind. It wuddn much, but then what the fuk was it? I mean, I *know* what it was—it was a lock of black hair tied with a red ribbon. And it was obviously a woman's. The question is what was that doing in there amongst all them other things? And why did he leave it? That part I can kind of figure out: he didn't know he wuddn coming back to the silo. Bone Face's lieutenants must've got him and give him to them Mo-fukkin-hammedans, who then took him over to Miss Helena's before he had a chance to say yeeow.

Too, he was probably oblivious to *things,* things in terms of possessions as such, anyway. I say that because I got the impression that's the kind of *nuts* he was.

I've asked around, and don't nobody ever remember anybody in his family with that kind of hair, and, for that matter, don't nobody ever remember anybody in the town or the county with that kind of hair. I sure as hell don't, and I've seen ever'body here for the last fifty years and know 'em by heart.

There are just so many loose ends to the whole episode. I guess I just didn't know what I was getting myself into when I decided to go after that sumbich. I didn't mean for it to become as important as it did. Basically, I figured I was out to have a little fun, and the thing ate my fukkin ass alive.

I couldn't see that I was no different than any other sumbich in my position. And he was a gotdamn menace to the community. You don't know what a crazy person is apt to do, especially if he's just running around loose, mostly at night, and don't nobody really know where he is. I mean that's that kind of situation I was dealing with.

Well, that's one way to look at it. The truth is I just wanted to shoot his ass, and I guess I can't really doll it up no better'n that.

Now, one thing about them notebooks—which you have already seen some of as we done gone along: That sumbich was having all kinds of fukkin halucinations, I guess. Otherwise, I don't know how else to explain the kind of goo-lala he wrote.

Plus, as you know, I kept them. I never did give them to nobody—hell, for one thing, nobody seemed to give a shit but me. So I kept them all these years, and occasionally I get them out and ponder them a little bit. He *was* crazy. Check this:

> The path and the high water are one,
> each an aspect of the same thing – time, of course,
> whose liquid form is the high water
> and whose firmness is in the path,
> which I may have found,
> though I have not been able to be perfectly certain.
> Otherwise, time is a gas
> whose particles cannot be nabbed,
> even by those who need them.

What a pile of crap. Don't none of it make any sense, even though some of it sounds like the Bible—well, maybe not exactly, but you know what I mean. It's like stuff some muthafukka in a *robe* would say.

> But, other than certainty, something else is lacking. This not-so-ancient tower would be complete if I had now the company of a beautiful girl. But I do not think it should be Kimbrough. No. Her last name is "Towers." Kimbrough Towers in a tower is a bit too much. She belongs in Memphis or, possibly, Sweetbriar. All the old ladies said she had skin like alabaster.

> No, thank you.

> Really, I think the girl should be Ahni, the quarter-Choctaw, whose father, for a time, was bookkeeper at the oil mill.

We were fourteen, for a time,
and held hands, for a time,
in the Mythic Theater
at the matinee
one Sunday,
in the Sunday dark,
and she was dark –
certainly nothing there that could even
faintly be construed
as alabaster.

*I want the darkness and the soft skin of the girl I loved that
Sunday afternoon at the picture show. (No alabaster, please. I
cannot be in love with blondes. My eyes are blue enough.)*

Yes –
we now would touch like rain and light,
and kiss while the Devil beats his wife.
I am fond of kissing, lips and tongues that speak
in hot synapse
to fire the heart with meaning
and flood the soul
with sudden glory on the skin.

Oh,
*the skin: It is not a cover but a silk to bring the inside out,
the organ of true communication, and I can say quite frankly
that home will not be home for me without the beauty of the
girl's dark hand*
upon my skin again.
So
Let Memphis dance away the night

and walk through arbors
of indoor orchids in my absence.
I have always known I would not be missed.
What's one more tuxedo in a sea of ice?

When Voyd seen that right there, he squinted up at me and said, "Junior Ray, do not ever let Sunflower get a'hold of this shit, man, or she will leave my ass and hunt the muthafukka down herself, and I won't never see her again."

And I said, "What the fuk are you talking about? That googah don't make a gotdamn bit of sense."

And he said, "Asshole, don't nothin' have to make sense to a woman hooked on love."

And then he explained that all Sunflower did, at that time, was read them love books. "And this crap sounds exactly like 'em," he said, "except this stuff was wrote by a real man and not by some fukkin book writer, and, crazy or not, she'd be after him on all fours in a jiffy."

"I guess," I said to Voyd, "'bout all y'all ever say to each other now is 'Pass the peas.'"

"Yeah," he come back, "but if I could say crazy shit like what's wrote in them notebooks, she'd pass 'em to me. As it is, though, I have to get up and get 'em mysef."

"Pretty bad," I said, "when a sumbich can't get pussy nor peas neither. Sounds to me then like you might have to be doing some other stuff for yourself, 'cause it looks like sex with Sunflower's done gone to seed."

That was a joke. But Voyd got all pissed off and said, "Fuk you, Junior Ray! But, yeah, that's how it's done got to be, and I ain't happy about it, neither."

"Well," I said, "*some* good has come of you bein' married."

He allowed it had but, as he put it, "Bein' married has

helped me make more of mysef that I would have otherwise, but marriage was the death of romance."

I guess Voyd had a point. If Sunflower had rather read about love in books instead of actually doin' it and makin' trips to Meffis, like she used to, with her underpants in her purse, that means the world was changing even more than I thought. On the other hand, I really believe both of 'em wanted to still "do it," but Sunflower just didn't want to do "it" with Voyd no more, and I wouldn't have either, if you want to know the fukkin truth. Anyway, because she had done got a little older, she didn't feel like makin' the effort to go elsewhere.

And Voyd, if I know that little sumbich, he was probably just as happy fukkin his fist—while at the same silly-ass time believing he'd be all tore up if Sunflower was to leave him. But she wouldn't have. By then they'd got too much tied up together, and she didn't want to lose none of it. And I'll guaran-fukkin-tee you both of 'em will be up there in that big kingsize bed eat'n and fart'n, with her reading about love and him watchin' the ballgame, and they'll live thatta way until some sumbich turns the TV off.

'Course, the truth about Sunflower was pretty well summed up by old Dr. Wilkins who said, when she was born, he had to get the lies out of her mouth before she could breathe.

8

Morse Code — I Feel Unfulfilled — Eye-Fukkin-Talians & Other Foreigners — My Sex Plan Involving a Preacher's Wife — The End

But, now, this next thing Leland Shaw wrote in his notebooks kind of gets to me. During the time that that stuff I've been telling you about was going on, and we was chasing around trying to find that crazy fool, there was that day I mentioned earlier when Mr. Hopper down at the depot called the Sheriff's office and said somebody was out there somewhere messing with the telegraph wires on the railroad.

He said his "key" was acting funny and that he was getting messages he couldn't make no sense out of—oh, he said he could *read 'em* just fine, it's just that they didn't have no connection with the railroad or with nothin' else that he could think of. This went on for a while and interfered with the runnin' of his station.

The weird-ass thing is that the radio in the patrol car behaved kinda peculiar, too, about the same time, and so this next part of Shaw's notebook writing is what reminded me of that time. And, if you want to know the truth, it kind of makes my skin crawl, because what he says is what Mr. Hopper said was coming over the telegraph wire, and I reckon the dah-dits Voyd and me was hearing on the patrol car's radio might have been the same thing, but I'll never know because I didn't know no morse code at the time. I do now, a little bit, because I finally got roped into helpin' out the Boy Sprouts for a couple of years.

Anyway, one day, for no visible reason the two-way in the patrol car started cracklin' with all this static—and they weren't no storm comin' neither.

Voyd said, "Junior Ray, this radio's all fukked up a-gin!" And I said, "Hotdamn, I told 'em to fix that thing."

And then Voyd said, "Sounds lak it's pickin' up some kyne-uh telegraph signal—listen. . . ." So we bent down close to the speaker and through the fizz and the hissin' of the static, we could hear, plain as shit on a shoe, that dah-dah-dit of a code transmission.

"What's it say?" Voyd asked me.

"How the hell do I know, asshole. I ain't no Boy Sprout," I answered.

That stuff kept up for days, and Mr. Hopper told us it was sayin' all kind of crazy things, like "Mother, Father, I am fine. Wish you were here." And then it said a lot of stuff involvin' the army, like "Sarge, Sarge, are you still there?!" But some of the time it wuddn nothing but the alphabet, first forward, then backwards, and forwards again.

Mr. Hopper didn't have no trouble at all makin' out what the dah-dah-dits said, coming over his telegraph, and also over our radio, as well as the radios of one or two of the big planters who was the first, at that time, to put 'em in their cars and in their managers' pickups.

The day we asked Mr. Hopper to listen to the two-way in the patrol car, he said, "It reads: 'I'm okay. Don't know coordinates. Will try to locate you.' Sounds like somebody's lost, if you ask me."

I was so upset I hollered at him and said, "Well, where'nafuksit comin' from!?"

"Now, Junior Ray, I can't tell you that anymore than you can tell me, but if you-all've got the proper equipment, you might be able to get some kind of a fix on the transmitter; but, otherwise . . ."

"Crap," I said, "we'll have to ask Meffis."

Well, as I mentioned, there was a great deal of crackle and pop which went along with the dah-dah-dits, and it made radio communication, not to mention the telegraph, all over Mhoon County pretty nearly impossible.

So that's why this that I'm going to show you really shook my tree. I can't explain it, but that don't mean it can't be; anyhow, here it is:

After having been out much of the night foraging for food, I went to sleep one morning about nine o'clock practicing my morse code. I had never used it; however, I have always regarded it as a useful means of communication, so I began my exercises by tapping messages with the middle and index fingers of my right hand – even though I am, in fact, left handed – upon a small block of wood I found buried in the seeds, at the top of the silo, on the first day of my occupancy, after I had settled into what became the most comfortable of nests.

My messages were addressed to Sergeant Crawford, my company "top," to-wit: "Dear Sergeant Crawford," I tapped, "it seems I am lost." And then I went on to say, "If you receive my transmission, please respond." My thinking was that the exercise might help me orient myself. In fact, I concluded my message to Sergeant Crawford by saying, "Perhaps if I can describe my surroundings, you will be able to help me, at least, to return to the unit, although home is where, mainly, I have in mind to go."

I believe I can safely say that practicing one's morse code is a sure cure for insomnia, for, at that point, I fell sound asleep.

After a time, around noon, I awoke, awakened because my fingers were tapping ever so gently upon the wooden block. But this time I wasn't sending messages: I was receiving one! "Lieutenant," the message read, "Lieutenant, what is your position?" It was from Sergeant Crawford.

I answered immediately. "Dear Sergeant Crawford, I do not have the slightest notion what my position is, but, it is good to know that, though unlocatable, or perhaps unlocated, I am not entirely alone." He responded by saying, "Lieutenant, can you describe your surroundings? Find a landmark which I can locate on my map. That way I can guide you to us." I answered by saying, "There is land, but there is no landmark unless I am occupying it. I am resting comfortably beneath the roof of a very tall silo which stands right in the middle of a plain, broken by bits of forest and swamp. One direction looks like another, except the view to the west, and there I see a railroad track. However, I have not yet observed or heard any trains go by. Does this help?"

"Not at all," said Sergeant Crawford. "That could be any-where." And, then, he went on, "Sir, we, ourselves, have not seen the enemy for quite some time, though I shall say we feel there are patrols in the area. Yet, it is difficult to defend ourselves when we are never attacked. The war has become very strange. Please reply."

I did and transmitted, "Dear Sergeant Crawford, I am glad to know the shelling has stopped. It was during the worst of it that I seem to have gotten separated from the unit, and

*though, as I have said, it is my intention to go home, I would
very much like to rejoin you, at least long enough to get my
bearings so that, then, I can finally go home. I am afraid going
home is my first priority, but I can tell you that you and the
platoon and, indeed, the cause, which, I confess, has slipped my
mind for the moment, are, without reservation, my second.*

*"The problem is I have lost track of time – or vice versa. I
cannot always tell the difference between a minute and an
hour, an hour and a day, a day and a month, and so on. Even so,
time has not become meaningless. Heaven forbid! Rather, it is
as though time has become mostly motionless or, maybe,
simply undetectable at the moment. I cannot say any of this
with certainty. It is more of a suspicion. Nevertheless, I don't
really know how long I have been lost. Yet I am sure of one
thing: if I can find the high water, my difficulty will be resolved."*

Now that's the kind of crap that Mr. Hopper had wrote
down that was coming out over his telegraph key, which, when
I think about them dah-dits Voyd and me was hearing on the
two-way radio in the patrol car, leaves me with a creepy-ass
feeling. This stuff and the thing about the footprints disappearing are the two elements in the whole episode that has always
made me think, as I have mentioned, that there was a lot more
to all of it than just what it seemed to be at the fukkin time—like
maybe God was involved, or somethin'. There is definitely
somethin' unnatural about it, and, bein' unnnatural, well, that
could mean God was messin' around with the natural way of
things on a more or less local level, if you know what I mean.
Plus, if you believe in the Bible, then you know that's the kind
of thing that went on back then. The only difference is we don't
wear a bunch of robes and ride around on jackasses, and if
there's any shepherds around here this day and time, them sheep

better watch out. Whoa, I got to fart—quick, pull my finger!
'Course, there ain't no more sheep neither. Everything's changed,
except me.

It may be necessary to write The Sacred Book of the
Choctaw. As is customary with most such books, I shall invent
every word of it, and begin it, to wit:

The world began in the egg of the marsh hawk.
From it came the hardwood and the cane, the cypress,
and all the grasses and vines, flowering, as it were,
like the golden yolk, all unto the reaches
of the formless void
between here and Memphis.

Nevertheless, some time after the Choctaw had moved
away and, in fact, even after a time itself was gone , the little
houses of the possible Africans
squatted in the fields like skulls,
their empty history,
scattered by the present,
siteless,
and covered by vines.
The evidence was disappearing, of both time and Choctaw,
written steadily into oblivion with invisible events, devoured
further by the iron bugs of progress and pollution that crawled
across the fields ingesting the nineteenth century
and excreting profits
unrecognized and unheeded
in their own country.

Therefore, I must search for Iboes yet be careful not to

trust my life to false Mandingoes – these watchmen, who disguise themselves as Negroes, may, in fact, be Germans at play on some sort of nordic holiday. I shall watch their step and elude them if I can; still, it is the tall, skinny Caucasian and his short friend who seem the ones to avoid. Those two may or may not be Germans, but I can see clearly that they are Nazis.

THAT STUFF JUST DRIVES ME FUKKIN WILD. I don't understand one coksukkin word of it, and, at the same cotton-picking time I can't bring myself to th'ow it away—I guess because it keeps me in contact with that sumbich, even if it's what you call only psycho-fukkin-logicially. And I have learned about bullshit like that from watchin TV.

Besides, it's a piece of unfinished business I ain't ready to let go of. I was talking to a muthafukka the other day, and he was pissing and moaning about how he never did get his college degree. I said, "Fukyew; I got things I never did finish either, and I ain't out here pissing and moaning about 'em." Hell, I told the coksukka, life's got to go on.

Christ, as far as I'm concerned, my life was ruint that day when Sheriff Holston come up to me and said to stop chasing that crazy-ass Leland Shaw. Oh, I reckon I could have kept on trying to find him, but I didn't have a pot to piss in, and I didn't have that kind of time off. You've got to be rich if you want to shoot some sumbich clear across the country. And what if I had gone up to Chicago looking for that asshole? Can you see me blending in with all the niggas? I'da stuck out like a redheaded stepchild at a family reunion. Plus, if that gotdamn Voyd had'a been with me, I know what would've happened; we'da wound up eating barbeque with them coksukkas and talking about hunting fukkin rabbits back in the gotdamn South. I ain't never seen it fail. Them muthafukkas have a way about 'em that defeats the piss out of me, and I admit it—well, *now* I admit it; it took me a fukkin lifetime, but now I do admit it. And I still don't understand it neither.

On the other hand, the way I see it, just 'cause, from time to time, them sumbiches is smarter than me, don't mean they're better than me. Plus, you never know what the real truth *is* about 'em. I mean, them sumbiches is worse than a politician. For instance, the story was out all over town that Bone Face's oldest grandson went out to Hollywood and made a big fukkin success as an *actuary*, but I don't believe a gotdamn word of it because I ain't never seen him in one single fukkin movie, unless he's playing in them special black films, but I wouldn't be looking at them no way.

Anyhow, that's how they are: partly what you hear, partly what they tell you, partly what you believe—partly what is and what ain't, and you'll never know the real truth. Sometimes I don't even think they *are* real, like I just made 'em up, or I'm just dreaming them or something. Only, once in a while, I think it's the exact opposite and that it's them that's dreamin' me. Now, here's the last little bit of them notebook pages out of the stack I let you look at—you might as well th'ow some of them in too and be fukkin done with it:

> I would know the Delta anywhere.
> Summer, for instance,
> Summer was there.
> And in the silence of its heat,
> sound itself was consumed and cooked and so sank,
> perhaps, directly into the earth
> beneath the shoes of those who occasionally
> dared to walk along the melting street,
> where, really, only the passing

of wagon wheels prevailed,
while all the rest was image only,
yet slow and suspended,
like swimmers in a dream.

When Fall came
with dry, slanted light,
smoke rose in yards along the street from school
where girls appeared and moved as though the air itself,
had made them;
all this after stars fell in showers
and drove away the dampness and the heat,
cooled the midnight air with darker flame,
and made the morning smell of promise.

Then Winter stepped in
with cold, cold feet
and clear blue eyes that shot the narrow light that burned
the grass, stripped the trees, and called the harrier to the fields
to glide, on patrol, swift and low above the sedge and over the
little dry-brown stalks of former cotton that rattled in the
wind.

But thoughts – ah, thoughts! – they scamper like mice,
back and forth, inside my head where some, I think, hide low
and lost beneath the gray, forgotten static of another time.

To find them, I must call upon the hawk, so that I may see
once more, and clearly, that cerebral landscape I am trying
desperately to paint and in so doing to discover it again.

Perhaps what is most frightening of all is the possiblity

that what I am looking for was only an impression in the first place and not a real place at all.

That well could be. I am a traveler without options. The myth is all I've got. But I shall find the past alive in future tents.

Goodbye, Dostoyevski. Goodbye.

I DON'T KNOW WHO THE FUK THAT IS—sounds to me a little like a sumbich that run a drygoods store down in Clarksdale, who used to tell the niggas his name was "Sweet Jesus." They'd all go on about how they was gonna go down to "the Sweet Jesus store" on *Sair'dy*, but, of course, back then they didn't have sense enough to know Jesus was a white man and not no Jew. But Shaw knew him, way back.

People said Leland Shaw, when he was a lot younger and before he went off to Dubya-Dubya Two, liked to hang out with all *kinds* of foreigners—I'm talking about Chinese, and I mean all of 'em in ever' coksukkin lil' ol' grocery store between here and Mound Bayou since 1882, plus the fukkin Syrians (and it's a fact all them sumbiches are kin just like the niggas and planters), and he sure as shootin' knew all them Eye-fukkin-talians we got in the Delta (Hell, in two of them towns down Highway 61, the whole gotdamn football team's got a' Eye-talian name)—and on top of that he didn't go to church like he should have, and so they knowed all along, way back yonder, that there was something *not right* with his ass.

But, even though he could play the piano and was what you might call close to his mother, he wuddn no sissyboy, and that's one reason I figured folks *ought* to have been scared of him when they found out he was running around loose. They already knowed he was certifiable crazy when he come home and didn't believe he was here.

His early behavior plus his genuine insanity after the war was to my advantage. I pretty much believed he was harmless, but I hoped everybody else would think he was dangerous. And I almost did a few things that would have been pret-ty fukkin awful just so I could lay the blame off on Shaw. For instance, at the same time all that was going on, some sumbich who was walking down 61, on his way around the world, pulling a little wagon he slept in, had a heart attact right out on the highway by the Ford place—then St. Leo had a Ford place and a Chevrolet place, plus at one time we also had a Pontiac place and a Plymouth dealership, which was pretty fukkin amazing for a town of only twelve hundred people, although you have to remember it was also the county seat, and they was around twenty thousand people in the town and county combined, understanding, naturally, that only about two thousand of 'em was more or less white.

Anyway, we couldn't find out nothin' about the man, so Sheriff Holston told me to see that he got buried. Well, I had about decided that, before I put him in the box, I was gonna cut off one of his fukkin arms and cook it, so it would keep better, and then I was gonna take it out across't the levee and stick it on a spit over a cold campfire, and, later, not too much later so that some fukkin animal wouldn't grab it, I was gonna have it *discovered* by me and, I guess, Voyd and one or two other dumb sumbitches, and make it appear Shaw was out there killing folks and eat'n 'em.

I never did do it, but I sure as hell thought about it, and now I know I should have. Well, that's hindsight for you.

But there was more. I knew that if I could get the women scared, the men would all step into line and want the sumbich put out of his misery in a fukkin hurry. So, I said to myself, what was the worst, most awful coksukkin crime that could be committed besides murder and cannibalism? And, then, it come to me: *sex*.

In Mhoon county, you can blow some asshole's head off with a shotgun, and nobody, except a few of his immediate family, will hate you for it; but pull out your dick, and even Jesus hissef can't save you—and *wouldn't*. . . if he gave a shit about his reputation around here.

So, risky as it was, I made up my mind I was gonna go to Meffis and get a wig and a fake beard, so nobody would know who I was and so I would look like that wild-ass Leland Shaw. Still, all that was just background, so to speak, for the real point of the thing I was gonna do— And that was more connected to the fact that somebody, once, had a company from California send me a catalog of all kinds of weird stuff, "marital enhancers" and the like, and in it was a couple or three advertisements for enormous rubber you-know-whats. They looked real, too, and e-fukkin-normous like Bobby Joe MacInerny's, which he used to swing backwards between his legs and piss from the middle of the boys' locker room all the way to the gotdamn pee-trough when we was playing football back in high school. It was bigger than a mule's.

Bear in mind, I hadn't never seen nothin' like the kind of stuff that was in the catalog I told you about, 'cause we didn't yet have it around this part of the world, naturally, as they do now up in Meffis. Anyway, suddenly I seen a use for it. And I ordered off for one.

My plan was to outrage the whole fukkin town, and the way to do that, I figured, was to wait until a Tuesday night because that was when they had the Town's Board of Supervisors meeting, and Brother Weathercraft, the Baptist preacher, would

be there, because he had been named an honorary member of
the board, just like the Methodist preacher and the Presbyterian
one, only they never went to the meetings except when it was
their time to give the prayer (now, the Episcopals didn't have a
preacher because there was so few members, and they had to get
one down from Meffis from time to time), but Brother
Weathercraft went to every single meeting because, as he said, he
felt it was a way to show Christ in action—which meant that
Miz Weathercraft, Martha May, would be at home by herself.

And I have to say this: the reason I picked Brother and Miz
Weathercraft as the key to my sex plan was because it was a well
known fact that she, Martha May, had stood up in church and
told God and everybody else that her and the preacher wrapped
theysefs all over from head to toe in bed sheets whenever they
"sought to beget a child" so that their "sinfulness would be more
acceptable in the sight of the Lord."

Another reason was that, unlike the other two preachers, the
Weathercrafts didn't live next to the church but had a house
provided for them a little way out of town past the Irish Ditch.
It was just enough removed from things to give me the privacy
I needed.

Here was the deal: I was going to go up onto the porch,
wearing the wig and everything I'da bought from the joke shop
in Meffis and have this big-ass two-foot-long, warty-looking
rubber whonker sticking straight out of my britches. Then I'd
ring the doorbell, and when Martha May come to see who it was
and flicked on the porch light, there I'd be, standing there with
that mail-order whang, wangling it around right there in front
of her—I don't know what I'd 'a done if it had fell off! I couldn't
of left it layin' on her porch. Hell, my fingerprints woulda been
all over it.

It was a whale of a good idea. But, I never did do it.

Something would have gone wrong, and I'da been locked up in Parchman to this very day . . . if I was lucky.

The whole thing was just too risky. I thought about getting Voyd to do it, but I felt the sensitive nature of the issue demanded that nobody but me know about it, and, of course, Miz Weathercraft. And, too, I was a little bit afraid she'da looked at me and said, "Junior Ray, what the fuk are you doin'?," not that those would have been her exact words.

Now, how could I have answered that?

I suppose I'da said, "I ain't Junior Ray, I'm Voyd," and run off. I don't know. But, I do know it was probably the best thing that I didn't never do it.

It *is* possible, however, that Miz Weathercraft, Martha May, coulda looked straight at that rubber dick, big as it was, and not seen it, if you know what I mean, because, you see, a dick is about the last thing any woman, much less a preacher's wife, around here ever would expect to see, and I imagine they's a lot of wives right here today that have never even seen one because they probably always did it in the dark, so there is a huge possibility that Martha May, Miz Weathercraft, wouldna known what it was sticking out of my britches that way unless she'da reached out and grabbed it.

Which means she'da gotten hold of the evidence. And I'da been done in by a blunt instrument.

But I guess it's like they say; the Lord looks after little children and assholes, and I've always seemed to know which way to jump. Plus, I guarantee you I never thought I'd be set'n up here having nobody write down my memwars.

But every time you turn around, some sumbich is knocking on doors wanting to learn about the South and especially about the Delta.

Every bit of it is true, too. The fact is that even with the changes, the South is real, and it's all the rest of the fukkin country that's been invented.

But just because a place changes, it don't mean it's gone. Naturally, all these things I'm remembering took place before the changes came. The stuff I've told you about happened when we all still lived in the old way.

But, I guess, within half a dozen years later, everything was different . . . except, of course, me.

I find that I am desperate to believe the unbelievable

Anyway, even if Leland Shaw hadn't never been drove nuts in the war, he was always known for having his head in a book, which is a sure sign something is wrong with your ass; and, as I have said before, even though everybody down here in the fukkin Delta is crazy in one way or another, people in the lower Delta don't mind it, but these coksukkas up here in the upper part all disapprove of it, which is pretty strange because they're crazy, too; and, if that's so, then, to my way of thinking, it's like they don't approve of themselves—which is the craziest part of all.

A fellow down in Greenwood said he believed the difference in the lower and the upper Delta was that the lower part was focused on New Orleans, and the upper part was glued to Meffis and that it was all them Scotch-Irish muthafukkas up here, as opposed to all them Frenchies down yonder, that determined how people saw theysefs.

I know one thing. You can have a helluva lot better time in New Orleans. Shoot, down there you can walk in the middle of the street with nothing on but a condom, and if somebody looks at you funny, all you have to do is say, "Thought it might rain," and they won't pay you any attention at all.

But try that in Meffis . . . well, there, you'd probably get off a lot lighter if you didn't wear the condom.

. . . The myth is all I've got. . . .

I GOT A PISTOL ON MY HIP I been carryin' for over thirty-five years, and I ain't yet got to put it to the use it was intended. People say, "Gotdamn, Junior Ray, why didn't you just shoot you a nigga?" And I tell them, "Fukyew, sumbich, I don't want to shoot no nigga." I didn't then, and I don't now. Hell, anybody coulda done that. I do have some fukkin pride, and I wanted to shoot a muthafukka that would count for something—Hell, I wanted to kill a gotdamn white man. I mean, what's the sense in wasting your buckshot on rabbits?

Leland Shaw was my chance, and I missed it. If I'da caught up with him right at first, I coulda blowed his ass off and been a hero in the bargain, because, right there at first, there was a whole lot of folks that was more than just uneasy about him being loose out there somewhere; they was a good many of 'em that was just plain scared, and I coulda been the one to save 'em from the maniac. But all that changed as time went on, and people started wanting to save *him.*

If you've ever dealt with the public, you know what I mean. Anyway, it was a damn shame, and it's been a great fukkin sadness in my life.

Epi-Fukkin-Logue

AND ONE LAST THING, MUTHAFUKKA. JUST BE SURE YOU PUT all this down like I told it. You hear? 'Cause I dont want to have to add your ass to my list. Move, I got to spit; and I ain't got my cup.

ABOUT THE AUTHOR

JOHN PRITCHARD grew up in the Mississippi Delta. He teaches college English in Memphis, Tennessee. *Junior Ray* is his first book; NewSouth Books released the sequel, *The Yazoo Blues*, in 2008.

JUNIOR RAY RETURNS IN

The YAZOO BLUES

by JOHN PRITCHARD

"John Pritchard again indulges the profanely backwoods, occasionally backwards, voice of Mississippi 'good ol' boy' Junior Ray Loveblood. [Loveblood's] account of a failed Union naval expedition at Yazoo Pass on the Mississippi River also includes the story of his research expedition, with his friend Mad Owens, to the Magic Pussy Cabaret & Club 'up in Meffis.'

"Each interwoven story is as surprising and strong as Junior Ray himself, who conjures a surreal scene of ironclads logjammed in a bayou as colorfully as he recounts a backroom lap dance from his best friend's granddaughter Petunia. Between expletives and misanthropic digressions, Junior Ray reveals a lifetime of deep, unlikely friendships, even getting at an occasional truth in a humble manner that's—as Junior Ray might put it—'as soft as a quail's fart.'" — *Publishers Weekly* starred review

"Darkly comic, profound and original, *The Yazoo Blues* stakes out Pritchard's territory on the rough side of Southern Literature."
— WILLIAM GAY, *Twilight*

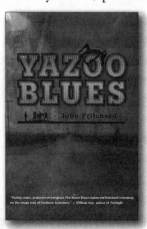

ISBN 978-1-58838-217-7
256 pages • $24.95

Available from your favorite bookstore or online at
WWW.NEWSOUTHBOOKS.COM/
YAZOOBLUES